Also by Mary Behan

FICTION

A Measured Thread

NONFICTION

Abbey Girls
(with Valerie Behan)

KERNELS

Stories

MARY BEHAN

Laurence Gate
Press

You can contact the author at mvbehan.com

Publisher's Cataloging-in-Publication Data
Names: Behan, Mary, author.
Title: Kernels : stories / Mary Behan.
Description: Mazomanie, WI : Laurence Gate Press, 2021.
Identifiers: ISBN 978-1-73449-434-1 (paperback) | ISBN 978-1-73449-435-8 (ebook)
Subjects: LCSH: Short stories. | Friendship--Fiction. | Self-actualization (Psychology)--Fiction. | Aging--Fiction. | BISAC: FICTION / Short Stories (single author) | GSAFD: Short stories.
Classification: LCC PS3602.E33 K47 2021 (print) | LCC PS3602.E33 (ebook) | DDC 813/.6--dc23.

LCCN: 2021909760

Cover and interior design by CKBooks Publishing
◆ ckbookspublishing.com

Laurence Gate Press
6383 Hillsandwood Rd
Mazomanie, WI 53560

For Val

Table of Contents

Dangerous Building

It was a spur-of-the-moment decision. My flight from Dublin to Gatwick was cancelled abruptly, together with all flights from Ireland to England for twenty-four hours. Something to do with Brexit. Attending the three-day conference had been worthwhile, but I was anxious to return to London to prepare for a series of important business meetings. I had enough memories of the city to last a lifetime and an extra day held little attraction. Irritated at the prospect of a wasted day, I marched through the hotel lobby to the elevator, mentally composing emails. Slowed for a moment by a porter pushing a luggage cart, the yellow-on-black logo of Hertz caught my eye and within a few minutes I was holding a set of car keys and a map.

Puffy white clouds skittered across the sky as I navigated towards the outskirts of the city. It took almost an hour to reach the ring road where I would have to make a decision, north or south. With no particular destination in mind, I followed the sun and found myself heading southwest on the motorway towards Cork and Limerick. I consoled myself with the thought that at least I was doing something and dismissed the niggling guilt of my growing carbon footprint. Lulled into a semi-daze by endless green fields and hedgerows, I wasn't paying attention when an exit sign with the name of the town where I spent my childhood whizzed by. The realization that it had been well over thirty years since I'd last been there came as a shock. For several more miles, the phrase "If not now, when?" nagged at me, but ultimately it was a call of nature that steered the car off the motorway at the next exit.

Leaving the convenience store, I had a rough idea of the direction I should be driving to get back to the village, but was soon lost in a spider web of narrow, winding roads flanked by tall hedges. All of a sudden a pair of imposing wrought iron gates interrupted the wall of green, triggering something in my memory. I pulled over, found a place to park, and walked back along the narrow lane. The gates were padlocked and a no trespassing sign hung lopsidedly from a piece of rusted wire wrapped around one of the railings, but it was easy enough to climb over a crumbling stone wall around the derelict gatehouse. I knew this place.

Following the deeply-rutted tracks that led through a grassy field towards a copse of rhododendron, I couldn't help feeling a child-like sense of excitement. Here I was, a respectable businesswoman in my mid-fifties, having an adventure. A sign, hanging from a rope slung across the driveway where it curved to the left, took me aback. Flanked by red warning triangles and exclamation points, it read "Dangerous Building - Keep Out."

An avenue of beech trees stretched ahead, their limbs curving gracefully over the gravel track. The house, when it finally came into view, was a shock. Up to that moment I had been immersed in my childhood memories, but what appeared at the end of the avenue was nothing more than a decrepit ruin. The roof had fallen in and one of the chimneys lay in a pile of rubble. With fortress-like precision, each of the window openings had been filled with concrete blocks, their symmetry at odds with the rough-cut stone of the remaining walls. If an unsuspecting visitor was in any doubt, a blood-red "Keep Out" scrawled across the bricked-up entrance reaffirmed the hostility of this place.

I walked to the end of the house, avoiding chunks of stone that had fallen from the crumbling walls. Turning the corner, the brick archway to the stable yard was reassuringly undamaged and I passed underneath it without flinching. Weeds clogged the cobblestones, but the orderly row of stables and barns were surprisingly intact. The back of the house was in slightly better shape, perhaps because of a later addition in brick that seemed to have weathered the years better than the native stone. Looking upward at one of the boarded-up windows, a sudden flash of memory caused me to laugh out loud. Behind that window there used to be a bathroom with a huge pedestal sink, a rust stain marring its porcelain perfection. That was where we used to wash our hands before tea.

§

"I know a bad word," Mickey said, giving me a sly look.

He and I were standing side by side sharing a sink filled with warm, milky-grey water. His fingers brushed against mine as he searched for the bar of soap.

"Do you want to know what it is?" His eyes were wide with anticipation.

Being eleven, I didn't know any bad words. But as Mickey was the same age as me, if he knew one, then I wanted to know it too. I nodded my head.

"It's jism," he said triumphantly, and before I could ask what it meant, we heard his mother's voice from downstairs calling us to tea.

Mickey's mother—her maiden name was Caroline Plunkett—grew up in our village. The daughter of the local butcher, she married up—as they say in Ireland—to the nephew of the family in "the big house" a few miles from the village. Like many of the big houses built by the Anglo-Irish in the eighteenth century, this one had passed its prime. Nonetheless, it retained an aura of grandeur, and the family was still treated as gentry by the locals. The newlyweds left for The Argentine, as it was called in those days, where he was going to raise cattle. Sixteen years later Mickey's mother returned with three children in tow and moved into the big house where her aged and eccentric aunt-in-law now lived. There was no sign of a husband, and I overheard my father saying that the nephew had always been a bit of a boyo. Perhaps because she had grown up in our village, people were sympathetic and said little about her unexpected return, except that she had kept her looks. Her children were another story—unmannerly savages, according to some of the local shopkeepers. But to me and my sister they were exotic, and moreover, they lived in a mansion.

"The girls should cycle over there some afternoon," my father said during a noon-time family dinner a week earlier. "The daughter must be about their age. She'd probably like someone to play with."

He had grown up with Caroline and must have felt sorry for her. And so it was decided that he would drive us there the following weekend to be introduced. We would stay for tea and he would come back later to bring us home. That night, tucked into our bunk beds in the cramped bungalow where we lived, my sister and I speculated as to what to expect. A moat and a drawbridge, or perhaps turrets.

"Maybe they have horses," she whispered.

We routinely begged our mother to get us a horse, or even a dog, but she was adamant in her refusal. She had no time to look after animals.

The drive to the big house seemed to take forever that Saturday even though it was less than five miles from the village. With each turn the road narrowed until it was barely the width of the car. Tall hedges obscured the fields, and we craned our necks to see if we could catch a glimpse of the place. The car slowed and stopped at an imposing set of wrought iron gates. A man came out of the brick gatehouse, nodded to my father, and opened the gates for us to pass. To have a live-in gate keeper was new to us children and signaled that this was no ordinary house. The gravel crunched under the tires as we made our way slowly up a driveway lined with rhododendron bushes and farther on, a perfectly symmetrical avenue of beech trees. When the house finally came into view, my sister and I were in awe. Although it didn't have turrets or a moat, it was an impressive sight. Three bays, each with dormer windows, flanked the massive entrance, which was accessed by an imposing set of stairs. A carpet of green ivy covered the façade, hiding its blemishes; although to our eyes it seemed perfect. My sister pointed excitedly to a brick archway that was recessed slightly at the far end of the building.

"I bet that leads to the stables," she said.

Caroline Plunkett came out to greet us with her dark-haired, slender daughter trailing behind. Once introduced, the daughter was eager to show us around, leading my sister and me through a maze of rooms and corridors from the basement to the attic, all the while throwing out random bits of information. There were dungeons and a secret passage—now blocked up—that led to the river so people could escape. One of the rooms in the attic was haunted because someone had been locked up there and died. The west wing was out of bounds. Great Aunt Edith's studio was there. Neither my sister nor I knew what a studio was, but it sounded important. Her two brothers, Robert and Mickey, were still at boarding school in England, but would be coming home the following week. Her boarding school had finished a week earlier. And yes, there was a horse, but he was no good for riding.

Outside in the stable yard, a short-haired dog sidled up to her, squirming awkwardly.

"That's Bella. She's going to have puppies," she said, ignoring the dog as she led us to the walled garden.

Here too, amidst the overgrown privet and neglected greenhouses were stories. A pet bear used to live in the garden, she told us, chained to a wall. And there were still some peach trees. We were enthralled. We had never eaten a peach, much less petted a bear.

Tea was a revelation. At our house tea consisted of a boiled egg with bread and butter, or baked beans on toast. Mrs. Plunkett had baked a sponge cake that morning, which was perched on a raised, silver cake stand in the center of the table. She set down an enormous bowl of cream, fresh from their Jersey cow, and a jar of home-made raspberry jam. As we watched, she sliced the cake into thick wedges.

"Go on then, help yourselves while I go and make the tea," she said.

To our shock, her daughter promptly took a slice, smeared a generous dollop of jam on it, and dipped it into the bowl of cream before stuffing the whole concoction into her mouth. I glanced at my sister, who was as wide-eyed as I was, and immediately copied our young hostess. This magical place had no rules, or so it seemed to me on that first day.

The big house became our playground that summer. Each weekend my sister and I would cycle the five miles, chattering excitedly in anticipation of what adventures might await us. There were picnics in the rhododendron woods where Robert and Mickey made a fire to boil water for tea and we pretended we were cowboys. We helped bring in the hay, sitting atop the horse-drawn wagon, pretending we were ladies of the manor as we waved majestically to the indifferent cows. We played forts in the hay loft, teaming up to compete for the coveted triangular window at one end. Bella had her puppies, and I brought the smallest one home. Surprisingly, my mother made no objection. And then the adventure ended.

§

A man's voice interrupted my thoughts, shocking me back to the present. He sounded angry.

"Ye're trespassin'!"

There was a figure standing in the archway, leaning heavily on a wooden stick. He looked to be several years older than me.

"Didn't you see the sign? This place is dangerous."

He pointed with his stick towards a sign almost buried in the tall weeds at the side of the house. I shook my head.

"No, I didn't notice it. I was too busy looking around." I smiled, hoping to defuse the situation, and added, "I used to come here when I was a child."

He came closer and peered into my face, as if he should know me. I could almost hear the gears reversing direction as he probed the past.

"I remember you," he said finally with a nod. "You were the one that was blinded that day."

Sometimes a statement hits you like a punch in the gut. You find yourself winded, unable to respond, not just physically but mentally. My mind went blank. It's not that I had forgotten *that day*. Rather, I had managed to push it aside and in the intervening years, worked around it. I didn't want *that day* to define me. In my twenties I had the scar repaired by a plastic surgeon in America, and rarely did anyone notice the unseeing eye. If they asked, I had my stock answer: "I had an accident as a child," delivered with a reassuring smile.

I could see him focusing first on my left eye, then the right.

"That's the one, isn't it?" He said, his finger jabbing at my right eye.

I flinched and jerked backward, my hand involuntarily rising to my face. I expected him to apologize but instead he turned and began to walk away. I found myself following him, wanting to resume our conversation, such as it was.

"How...how did you know that...about my eye, I mean?"

He didn't slow down, and for a moment I thought he hadn't heard me. I shouted at his back.

"How do you know about my eye?"

His shoulders twitched and I could feel his indecision. Abruptly he stopped and turned to face me. I backed away from him.

"Don't worry," he said, "I won't hurt you. You were hurt enough here. We both were."

Maybe it was where he stood, framed by the stable doorway. Above his head I could see the triangular window of the hay loft with its border of red brick.

"You're...the son, aren't you? The son of the man who looked after everything here. He lived in the gatehouse."

I grasped for a name. "Kit Shannahan! You're Kit Shannahan's son."

Unsure what to say next, I gestured towards the stable behind him.

"Remember? We used to play forts there. We'd try to pull each other down from the top of the hay stack."

I smiled at the memory, but there was no answering smile from him. Instead, he blinked a couple of times, then sniffed and wiped a hand across his face. I still couldn't remember his name.

"I'm Jim Shannahan," he said, moving the stick to his left hand and holding out the other. "And you are—"

He said my name as we shook hands. I was surprised he had remembered it. There was an awkward silence, broken by both of us asking a question at the same time. He gestured for me to speak.

"I've thought about this place so many times. I used to love coming here. But after the accident, my mother wouldn't let us come back."

I looked at Jim, waiting to see if he had anything to say. His mouth tightened and he began to shake his head.

"It was a bad business altogether. *They* were a bad business, the whole lot of them."

I shrugged, not sure where this was going but wanting to preserve my childhood fantasy.

"The daughter was okay, and I liked the mother. She used to let us do anything we wanted. The older brother was a bit snobbish, but Mickey and I got on well."

"The mother was a piece of work." Jim spat the words out.

"What do you mean?"

He opened his mouth to say something, but stopped. He looked at me closely, then began to shake his head.

"You don't know, do you?"

When I didn't respond, he asked, "Do you remember that day?"

"I have some memories of it, I suppose."

The words came out of my mouth sounding guarded because I wasn't sure if I wanted to say anything more. I could feel the tension building as he waited for me to continue. I took a deep breath.

"I remember that it happened over there," I said, pointing to the archway.

"We had been playing, Mickey and me. He wanted to play forts, but my sister didn't come with me that day, so there wasn't enough of us. He went into the hay loft but came out immediately. He was angry. I remember he bent down, picked up something lying on the ground, and flung it against the wall. There was a clanging noise, and then...then a blinding flash in my right eye. It hurt and I began to scream. I heard him shouting 'Mama, Mama, you have to come. There's blood!' He kept on saying, 'I didn't do anything. It wasn't me.' Then his mother was there, prying my hands away from my face. I must have been bleeding because she wrapped something around my forehead and eye. After that it's muddled.

"Someone took me to the hospital and then my parents came. After that there were nurses and doctors, and people whispering around me. Then it was all over and I went back to school, but now I had a big scar and wore glasses and always had to sit in the front row, and the nuns were extra nice to me. The visits to the eye doctor continued for years. I got the scar fixed, eventually. I was tired of always having to hide it with make-up."

The look on Jim's face was a mixture of puzzlement and sadness.

"Don't you remember my father? He was there too. He took you to hospital."

I shook my head.

"It was his shirt she wrapped around your face. We got it back a week or so later and the blood was gone, so he still wore it. I hated that shirt. It reminded me of everything wrong in our lives."

I must have looked puzzled.

"He was shagging her." His mouth tightened. "That day, the day you were blinded, they were shagging in the hay loft. Mickey saw them. That's why they were there so quickly."

I took this in slowly, trying to merge it with the story I had kept in my mind for years. It fit. Why Mickey was upset, why he had flung the rusted hinge against the wall. It had ricocheted and hit me, splitting open my forehead. A screw protruding from the hinge punctured my right eye. Much later it was explained to me that the optic nerve had been damaged, and I would be blind in that eye for life. I can still see light and vague shapes, but not much else.

Jim was speaking again. "She was a bitch. She didn't care about my father. He was just a handyman, a convenience. Robert—the older son—used to take pleasure in the whole business. He'd sidle up to me and say, 'tell your father that Caroline wants him,' with a lecherous sneer. God, I hated him."

An image of Robert came to mind just then—a good-looking boy who must have been sixteen or so that summer. He had an air of someone who knows...just knows... and I always felt slightly uncomfortable when he was around. Now, I tried to imagine what it must have been like for Robert that summer, knowing his mother was sleeping with the hired hand. It would have challenged him on so many levels—the first-born son of a union between an Anglo-Irish gentleman and a peasant, watching his mother sliding back to her roots.

"What happened to them in the end?"

It was the question I could never ask my parents.

"They left. Went to England. I heard Robert went into the British army and got blown up in Northern Ireland during the Troubles. Good riddance."

I was about to say something when he spoke again. This time there was anguish in his voice.

"I think he loved her. It had been a few years since Mam died. Maybe he thought...that Caroline would marry him or something. I tried to tell him he was being a fool, but he didn't listen."

There was a long silence.

"And you?" I asked.

He gave a little snort. "I went to England at the end of that summer. Dad stuck around until the old aunt sold the place. The new owners didn't want him so he had to move out of the gate house."

I could see the muscles in his jaw tightening. He swallowed.

"A few days later he hanged himself in there." I followed his gaze to the hay loft.

I felt the breath leave my chest and wondered if it would ever come back.

"I'll be off now," he said turning to leave. "Be careful where you walk. Them walls could topple at any minute."

After he left I stood in the stable yard for a long time. Like Lot's wife, I had looked back and seen my memories turn to dust. Perhaps I did have an inkling that things were not as they seemed in the big house that summer, but I wanted so badly to belong there. It was a magical place, and I was a still a child.

I never did find out what jism meant.

Imagined Scenes

Ever since she read about it, riding the Trans-Siberian Railway from Moscow to Vladivostok had been on Jennifer Fowler's bucket list. She was fascinated by train travel, and no other rail journey promised such a bigger-than-life experience, chugging across that vast expanse of Asia, where a single color dominated the world map. She imagined a few days in Moscow to buy necessities for the ten-day trip, a final check of her paperwork, and then that electric moment as the train moved slowly out of the station, gaining speed through endless grey suburbs, and finally bursting free into a landscape that stretched for thousands of miles to the Sea of Japan. In her mind's eye each scene along the way had its own vivid color, smell, and sound. Endless forests and snow-covered steppes punctuated by remote train stations; the curious faces of Russian farmers pausing to stare at the speeding behemoth; the lurching carriage with a samovar steaming quietly in the corner; the smell of sweat and damp wool and urine and garlicky sausages.

Excuses came and went. At first it was money—never enough—but as her career progressed, time became the limiting resource. Her Chicago law office was small, and if she took more than two weeks of vacation, someone else would have to attend to her clients. Colleagues were always willing to pick up the slack for a wedding or an illness, but for anything else they tended to be less generous. And so the Great Railway Bazaar scenes faded gradually as the years went by.

This had been a particularly challenging winter for Jennifer. One of the attorneys in her office had slipped on the icy sidewalk early in December and broken both wrists, leaving her unable to work. Much of her caseload had fallen to Jennifer, who had little choice but to work fourteen-hour days, dragging herself home each evening through the relentless cold of a Chicago winter. By the time her colleague returned to the office in mid-February, Jennifer longed for a break from the grinding routine. That afternoon, as her client's voice continued to drone on in the telephone receiver, she allowed her mind to drift. This was the third phone call with this man in as many days. He is a needy man, she thought; someone who likes the sound of his own voice and doesn't seem to care that every minute of her time comes with a price.

Absentmindedly, she scrolled through her e-mails. Pausing as one caught her eye, she double-clicked on the link that opened to a brochure for a conference in New Orleans the following month. The topic was only tangentially related to her area of expertise, but it piqued her interest. Her gaze drifted towards the window again. Yesterday's snow was already melting, merging with the grey of the sidewalks. In the distance the L-train wound its way between buildings, looking for all the world like a model railroad. Perhaps it was the juxtaposition of those two images in her brain, but by the end of the phone call she had made a decision. She would go to the conference in New Orleans—by train.

§

The tiny sleeper compartment would have been cramped with two people, but as she was traveling alone, it felt spacious. Two comfortable seats faced each other in front of a large picture window, beneath which hung a folding table. The porter who showed her to her roomette had stowed her suitcase deftly in a corner of the compartment, assuring her that he would take it out later when he prepared the cabin for the night.

"My name is Joseph, ma'am. If there's anything you need, just let me know. You can press that buzzer or just walk towards the back of the train. You'll find me for sure."

His broad, toothy smile left her feeling safe.

Remembering those erstwhile Trans-Siberian dreams, she had brought a bottle of wine, and as soon as Joseph closed the compartment door, she opened it and poured herself a generous glass. The train lurched briefly, prompting her to grab both glass and bottle, but then it relapsed into a steady movement as it trundled out of Union Station and into the Chicago suburbs. A tiny spark of excitement rippled through her. Her desk was clear for the next few days and nobody expected to hear from her. She was free.

It was the absence of movement that woke her in the middle of the night. Drawing aside the curtain, harsh lights illuminated a railway yard, and for a moment she wondered whether something had happened. A derailment on the tracks ahead perhaps, or something more ominous? The app on her smartphone showed the train in Memphis, Tennessee, close to the Mississippi River. She listened for any sounds of alarm but the corridor was silent, so she went back to sleep, sliding down between crisp, white sheets and pulling the woolen blanket up to her chin. The next time she woke it was daylight and the view outside had changed dramatically. This was the hidden America—hamlets where trains no longer stopped, settlements that shouted poverty and abandonment. The train moved slowly through this blighted landscape, allowing her to imagine how her life might have been had she grown up here. A dilapidated shack, its wide porch cluttered with sagging chairs, a washing machine, and a stack of empty beer crates was a chastening reminder that not everyone had a chance to live the American Dream.

Joseph helped her with her suitcase as she alighted from the train at the Union Passenger Terminal in New Orleans. She thanked him sincerely, feeling a momentary pang of apprehension at the prospect of leaving his care. She reminded herself that she wasn't stepping off into a remote Russian city but, rather, a familiar American one. She straightened her shoulders and walked out of the station into the mid-afternoon sunshine. The unaccustomed feeling of warm air on her skin made her smile.

She decided to walk the eight blocks to the boutique hotel in the Warehouse District where she had made a reservation. Signs of post-Katrina recovery were everywhere, although little seemed to have been achieved in the three years since the hurricane. By comparison with Chicago, the city felt hostile, and she walked briskly, her roller bag rattling on the uneven pavement.

That evening she had an early meal at one of the more exclusive restaurants in the city. It was the sort of place that normally required a reservation, but by going early she hoped they would seat her. She dressed carefully for the occasion, and as she expected, the maître d'hôtel scrutinized her before seating her in a quiet corner of his dining room. Leaving a little over an hour later, she paused at a street corner to watch a scene playing out that could easily have been in a Hollywood movie. Two police cruisers had pulled up behind a battered-looking sedan, their lights flashing. The occupants of the car— two young black men—got out slowly and stood beside their car, waiting. Four police officers emerged from the cruisers, their bulky gear making the process slow and awkward. One of them approached the two men; the other three stood slightly at a distance, their hands on their guns. The tension was palpable. Jennifer watched in fascination, waiting for someone to make a move—a wrong move. She didn't notice the woman behind her and was startled when a voice spoke quietly.

"Perhaps we should watch from a little farther away. It might be safer. I think we're in the line of fire here."

Jennifer turned to see a tall, elegantly-dressed woman around her own age with vivid blue eyes and short blond hair parted to the side and slicked down, giving her a vaguely masculine appearance. She was very beautiful.

"Maybe you're right," Jennifer responded, giving the woman a warm smile.

It was true. A stray bullet could easily hit either of them or any of the bystanders who had also stopped to watch. The woman touched her arm gently and led her across the street to a safer vantage point. For the next fifteen minutes they watched the scene play out, exchanging comments as to what might be going on and speculating as to how it might resolve.

Suddenly, as if on cue, all six men got into their cars and drove away, the cruisers turning left and the sedan continuing on straight past the two women. The crowd of onlookers began to disperse, but the two women lingered and continued their conversation, which by now had progressed to the rehabilitation efforts that were being undertaken in the Warehouse District.

Jennifer was about to say goodbye when the woman said, "I have an apartment just around the corner. Would you like to come up for a glass of wine? We have a lovely rooftop garden; you can see the boats on the river."

She tilted her head to one side and looked inquiringly at Jennifer, the side of her mouth turning up slightly with the hint of a smile. There was an awkward pause.

"I'm sorry. I should have introduced myself earlier. Veva Kiuru."

She extended her hand and Jennifer shook it, offering her own name in exchange. The name sounds vaguely Polish, Jennifer thought, yet this woman didn't remind her of any of the Poles she knew in Chicago. Normally she would have refused an invitation like this, claiming an early morning meeting or some such excuse. But to her surprise, she found herself agreeing. Veva intrigued her, and the prospect of doing something totally out of character was exciting. Besides, she reasoned, it was still relatively early in the evening, and while her hotel room was charming, it offered little besides a large TV.

Five minutes later they arrived at a four-story red brick building that, from its outward appearance, had once been a warehouse.

"My husband bought the apartment soon after Katrina," Veva said as she punched in a code on the panel beside a pair of heavy, wooden doors.

"Nobody wanted to come downtown in those days so it was a bargain. We live across the lake—Lake Pontchartrain—but this place is convenient when we go to concerts."

Any sense that the building had once been a factory disappeared as the doors swung open and automatically closed behind them. After the busy street noise, the silence was striking. A faint perfume of some sweet-smelling flower, the name of which escaped Jennifer, hung in the air. The spacious, dimly-lit foyer ended at a marble staircase that angled upwards into shadow.

"You don't mind if we take the stairs, do you?" Veva asked. "There's an elevator but I prefer the exercise."

The apartment was on the top floor of the building and consisted of a spacious, high-ceilinged loft with a row of tall windows that spanned the whole length of one wall. Facing the windows was a galley kitchen, separated from the room by an island at which stood two high stools. A hallway led off the room, presumably to the bedroom and bathroom, Jennifer thought. Decorated in a minimalist style, the floors were of recycled lumber sanded to reveal the dark wood grain. An L-shaped sofa dominated the center of the room, strewn with cushions in muted colors. In the angle of the sofa stood a large glass coffee table, empty except for a pair of silver and bronze stirrups with an intricate Arabic design carved into their sides. Beside them lay a shield and sword, both equally stunning. An image of Genghis Khan flashed into Jennifer's mind, seated astride his horse and looking fierce and magnificent.

As she followed Veva towards the kitchen, she ran her fingers delicately over a slab of cream-colored wood supported by a complex arrangement of stainless-steel cables and posts that looked to be a writing desk of sorts. It felt like silk, the surface hardly registering on her fingertips. Pausing, she stared at the object on the desk, which she recognized as a Japanese suzuri, the ink stone nestled into an intricately carved dragon whose eyes were fixed upon a golden egg. Beside the suzuri lay a calligraphy brush. She looked over at Veva, who was watching her.

"It's very beautiful," Jennifer said, gesturing towards the room.

"I like beautiful things," came the response.

Jennifer watched as Veva reached upward to slide two wine glasses from the rack hanging above the island. The movement was fluid and practiced and despite her own petite frame, she felt awkward by comparison.

"Your name is very unusual. Is it Polish?" Jennifer asked.

"Finnish."

"What do you do...for work I mean?"

"I work for the government," came the reply, but something in Veva's tone seemed to discourage further inquiry.

"And you?"

"I'm a lawyer. We do mostly health care stuff...representing hospitals and clinics. The laws around health care are changing all the time."

Veva nodded. "You drink white?" she asked, opening the refrigerator. "I have red if you prefer."

"White would be lovely."

She took out a bottle of wine, glanced at it, and uncorked it with practiced efficiency.

"It's a New Zealand wine and a good one. I promise." Her blue eyes lingered on Jennifer for an extra few seconds. Then, with glasses and bottle in hand, she walked towards the hall.

"Follow me," she said without looking back and disappeared into a small passageway from which a spiral staircase led upward.

The rooftop garden was a surprise. Each of the apartments in the building had its own private space, separated from neighbors by tall, wicker partitions. On opposite sides of Veva's garden, a steel and glass wall allowed for an uninterrupted view of the New Orleans skyline. A trellis festooned with lush greenery covered much of the tiny space, shading a table and two chairs. Veva poured a generous measure into the glasses and offered one to Jennifer.

She raised her own glass. "To safety," she said, the corner of her mouth turning up slightly.

For the next two hours they talked. Veva was a good listener, prompting the conversation with thoughtful questions but offering little information about herself. Something about the rooftop—a sense of removal from the world—allowed Jennifer to open up in ways she never had before. Neither confessional nor therapy session, it felt more like a conversation with her inner self. She could hear the disappointment in her own voice as she talked about her divorce seven years earlier and the few men she had dated since. All the while Veva's intense blue eyes held her attention, and for some reason she couldn't explain, she found herself yearning to elicit that unique smile.

The temperature had dropped slightly, and the wine bottle was empty. Veva stood up, stretched her arms above her head, and arched her back. She walked to the rail and looked towards the river. Silhouetted against the darkening skyline, Jennifer thought she looked magnificent, like a character out of an Avengers movie—feline, predatory, powerful.

"Come join me," Veva said, turning around to look at Jennifer. Although it was said softly, it was a command not a request.

Standing side by side at the railing they stared into the distance, neither speaking. Then Veva turned towards her and gently stroked her face. The caress carried a question and at the same time an expectation. Jennifer held her breath, not certain whether she wanted the scene to progress. But her body had already decided. Starting between her legs, a warm ache made its way through her body, bringing a flush to her face.

Then Veva kissed her. Her tongue explored Jennifer's mouth, withdrawing to linger over her lips, then plunging greedily again and again. Jennifer could taste the wine on Veva's breath. She closed her eyes, and in her mind saw the scene unfolding in slow motion, like a drop of water creating gently expanding waves. She felt Veva's hand raise her skirt and slip down inside her thong. Pulling in her stomach a little to facilitate the gesture, she could feel herself getting wet. Veva's fingers found her clitoris and stroked it very slowly and gently. Jennifer moaned quietly as she moved her pelvis rhythmically against the pressure. The hand withdrew abruptly and she gasped as every cell in her body ached for this sublime feeling to go on forever. Veva's mouth was still on hers, her arm around her neck, holding her in a tight embrace. Then she pulled away, took Jennifer's hand in hers, and led her towards the stairs. At the bottom of the spiral staircase, Veva turned to her. She was smiling.

"Let me blindfold you."

Her eyes were bright, her mouth slightly open as if expecting Jennifer to refuse. But there was no protest. She slid the silk scarf from around her neck and held it out in her hands, like an offering. Jennifer took a deep breath and accepted, raising the scarf towards her face. Veva helped her tie the knot and whispered in her ear, "Trust me."

Jennifer could feel the warm breath followed by the tip of a tongue deftly probing her ear. A thrill of pleasure erupted in her core. There was a gentle pressure on her back pushing her forward, and instinctively she held her hands out in front of her. A finger caressed her outstretched palm, threading its way to her wrist and closing around it like a manacle. She felt a slight pull and allowed herself to be drawn into the bedroom. Like Alice falling down a rabbit hole she had no sense of what might happen next, but she was willing to give herself up entirely to whatever might unfold.

§

She knew Veva was gone as soon as she woke the following morning. It wasn't just the absence of sound; it was as if someone had sucked all the life out of the apartment. For a few minutes Jennifer lay there thinking about the previous evening. Her hand went to her crotch, which was still wet and slightly bruised. She rolled over on her belly, inhaling Veva's scent from the smooth sheet. Every fiber of her body craved the exquisite pleasure she had experienced the previous evening. This is what a drug craving must be like, she thought—a gnawing pain in her groin that begged to be satisfied. But there would be no antidote to ease her back into her previous life. She pushed the thought aside and got out of bed. In the living room, propped up against a tall glass of water, was a card-sized piece of cream-colored paper. The letter 'V' had been inscribed on it with a perfect brush stroke of black ink. She turned the card over but it was blank.

Jennifer made a final tour of the apartment, trying to sear every detail of the space into her mind. She reached out to touch the suzuri, tracing the dragon from tail to head, her fingers lingering on the golden egg. The calligraphy brush lay beside it, still slightly damp. She took the card and slid it carefully into her purse. Then, with a feeling of immense loss, she left, closing the door decisively behind her.

The next day was filled with people and presentations, welcome distractions for Jennifer as they served to keep a maelstrom of conflicting thoughts at bay. Up to now all of her sexual encounters had been heterosexual, and as she searched through scenes from her past, nowhere had she ever felt attracted to a woman. The evening with Veva had been more pleasurable than anything she had ever experienced. Although sex with her husband was satisfying, it had been unimaginative. None of the men she had slept with since her divorce had made her feel the way she had with Veva, and she wondered if it would change her life in any way. But this was something she didn't want to dwell on, at least not yet.

On the second evening of the conference, Jennifer arranged to have dinner with a friend from her law school days who was also attending the meeting. They hadn't seen each other since before her divorce and spent an enjoyable couple of hours catching up. After dinner he offered to walk her back to her hotel and she agreed, steering him on a circuitous route through the Warehouse District with the excuse of showing him the architecture. As they walked past Veva's apartment building, Jennifer stole a glance upward, but the windows were unlit.

On the final evening there was a cocktail party for the two hundred attendees in the ballroom of the conference hotel. Waiters carrying trays of canapes and glasses of wine wove their way expertly among the crowd. Jennifer stood at a tall bar table with a group of colleagues, not quite engaged with their conversation. Looking around the room at some of the now-familiar faces, her heart missed a beat. Staring at her from across the ballroom was Veva, a tiny smile lurking in the corner of her mouth. Their eyes locked for several seconds until the crowd closed in and Jennifer lost sight of her. She abruptly excused herself and rushed to the spot where she had last seen Veva, but she had disappeared.

The following morning Jennifer took an early flight back to Chicago and by mid-afternoon was seated at her desk. Looking out her office window later that afternoon as the light was beginning to fade, she watched as the L-train threaded its way through the commercial buildings. Closing her eyes, she allowed herself to remember, and as the scenes unfurled like flowers, a world of possibilities began to emerge.

All That Glitters Is Not Gold

Holland, 1977

September

ELLEN

He sits by himself in the restaurant, the same table always. He must have arrived a few days ago while I was in Amsterdam, because the English couple who are staying here don't know anything about him. They've been friendly to me, which is a big plus, considering up to now we were the only three white faces in the hostel. Now there's a fourth. When I first saw the place two months ago, it reminded me of my freshman dorm at Oregon State, but to be fair, it's more like a conference center. There's even a bar on the sixth floor. Most of the people staying here are from Africa, although I heard something that sounded like Arabic being spoken. A few are from Samoa because I asked a guy with a tattoo on his face if he was from Hawaii and he said no, but that tattoos are common in Polynesia. All of the residents are men. Me and the English guy's wife are the only two women in the place, and as she's spoken for, I get a lot of attention. I'm beginning to dread the social events the staff organize for us. Some black guy always comes up to me and asks if I am married. I usually reply that my husband is back in the States and misses me terribly. This is a lie, of course—I don't even have a boyfriend there. The next question is usually whether my husband minds that I am here alone. I wonder if they mean, does my husband trust me?

The project I'm working on at the University of Groningen came with room and board and a small stipend. I'd never been outside the US except for a school trip once to Canada, but that doesn't really count. The prospect of spending a year in Holland was exciting; I thought I could see a bit of Europe. At the very least, I expected the experience would look good on my resume when I got back to the States and started applying to graduate schools. So here I am, living in a hostel in a small town in northern Holland where there is absolutely nothing to do.

I think I'll talk to the newcomer this evening at dinner, bring my tray over to his table and ask him casually if I can join him. He's looks older than me but not by too much, ten years perhaps. He's good looking— six-feet tall I'd guess and very fit, with a moustache and hair that flops over his eyes when he looks down at the book that's always open in front of him. Does that mean he doesn't want company? Hmm. We'll see about that.

PETER

The food's quite good, actually. I had expected cafeteria fare: chips and baked beans and greasy burgers, but it's not at all like that. Maybe it's the international influence; after all, they have to consider the different cultures they are feeding. When Kees suggested I live here for the first couple of months while he worked on finding an apartment, I wasn't at all keen. A hostel, for God's sake. I made it clear when I wrote back to him that I was much too old to share a bathroom. In his next letter he explained that the hostel—officially the International Agricultural Center—was purpose-built to house scientists from all over the world who come to Holland to learn about the latest in animal husbandry, seed growing, irrigation... skills like that. He added that I would definitely have my own bathroom. The Dutch get it right when it comes to international development, unlike the Brits who believe the tattered remnants of their empire still owe them something. Kees is a good fellow. He loaned me a bicycle, although I said I could easily walk from here to the Institute each day. It's barely two miles, and it's only for a couple of months. I'll buy a car when Julia and the boys arrive.

Looking around the dining room, it's hard not to notice the sea of black faces. They seem to be a cheerful lot, though, probably delighted to escape from their hell-hole countries for a few months. The Dutch are so damn serious by comparison; they get on my nerves at times. Still, I can see why the Australian government encouraged me to take this sabbatical. The research group at the Institute is top notch—years ahead of what we have in Tasmania. Julia wasn't at all enthusiastic, but she came around in the end, especially when I told her it would be just the thing for the boys—broaden their horizons and all that. I left it to her to break the news they would be leaving their friends for six months. That's her job, after all; she's their mother.

The other three "whities" usually sit together in the dining room, a pudgy man and two good-looking blondes, especially the taller one. I know one of the women is married to him because when I requested a double room, the bloke at reception told me the Taylors were occupying the only double room they have. He was probably lying; it's ridiculous to think there's only one double room in this place. My single is barely the size of a closet, and the bathroom's a joke. You almost have to sit on the loo to take a shower. At least there's a bar in the hostel, and the barman is English so we have something to chat about. He was curious as to how I ended up in Tasmania, and we had a long discussion about what life is like in Holland, or "cloggieland" as I prefer to think of it. Those wooden clogs are everywhere—in gift shops, on t-shirts and billboards, and postage stamps. Clogs and tulips. You get tired of it quickly.

The taller blond is coming this way with her tray. This could be interesting.

JULIA

Damn you Peter! The bloody car won't start and the boys are going to be late for school. You were meant to take the car in to be checked before you left for Holland, but then that meeting in Canberra came up. I'll have to call Mum and see if she can collect them from school this afternoon.

Why did I ever agree to this sabbatical? I can hear Peter's voice in my head, that calm voice he uses when he's displeased with something I've done. He would remind me I managed perfectly well by myself for far longer than this after Jack died. What he doesn't understand is that then, the whole village took me under their wing. I was the new widow and everyone felt responsible for what happened. The boys were too young to understand—only that their Dad died and went to heaven when he tried to help someone in a burning house.

After we moved to Hobart to live with Mum, she looked after the boys while I found a job and tried to get on with my life. Thanks to her they were never late for school, their sandwiches already made and tucked into their satchels each morning. Her car always started. Then Peter swept into our lives. The perfect solution, everyone said, especially as the boys needed a father. He was handsome, educated, had a good job, and was willing to take on a bewildered widow with two young children.

November

ELLEN

Peter is amazing! He's interesting and funny and he's traveled everywhere. I don't mind that he's a little older than me; he knows so much about everything. He's okay in bed too. The first time was a bit awkward, but then we ended up laughing because my bed was so ridiculously small. He said it reminded him of doing it in the back seat of his sports car when he was a student in England. That's where he grew up. He went to college in Wales and afterwards emigrated to Australia. A land of opportunity, he says, not like England, a country he considers dull and constricting. He lives in Tasmania, which he says is better than the mainland because there's a lot to do outdoors year-round, like bicycling and hiking and rock-climbing. He works for the government; it sounds a bit like the Department of Agriculture in the US.

I told him about being propositioned by one of the Africans at the hostel. The guy asked me to dance at the Saturday evening social. I'd had a few glasses of wine so I agreed. We were dancing for a couple of minutes when he told me I had good hips. Then he asked, did I like children, and could I cook? What a hoot! I told him I was an okay cook, but definitely didn't like children. He seemed so disappointed, but at least he and his friends left me alone after that. Peter and I had a good laugh. He calls the African guys "darkies," which makes me a little uncomfortable. Still, we laugh at a lot of the same things, especially the Dutch or "cloggies" because of the Dutch being famous for wearing wooden clogs, but that was a long time ago. We're going to The Hague next weekend for three nights. Finally, we'll have a proper double bed.

I think I might be falling in love with Peter. I think about him all the time and imagine what life would be like with him.

PETER

Well, she certainly makes this temporary housing situation manageable. She's fun to hang out with, if a little wide-eyed and immature. Typical American. All the same, she's got a great body. Yesterday I saw her in the bicycle parking lot; she was bending over to tie her shoe lace and I had to concentrate on not getting an erection. It wouldn't do to be seen staring at her—not in that state. The weekend in The Hague should be very enjoyable. I suppose I'll have to tell her about Julia soon, but there's no point in spoiling things just yet.

December

ELLEN

How could I have been so stupid? I just assumed he was single; he never gave me any reason to think otherwise, and he wasn't wearing a wedding ring. I suppose I should have asked. But if he had told me the truth, would I still have slept with him? Probably. But I wouldn't have let myself get so involved. I wouldn't have fallen in love, dreamed about spending our lives together. God, this hurts. I should have seen the signs, but I was totally head over heels and thought he loved me too. Why doesn't he love me? What's wrong with me? I want to curl up and die.

It did seem a little weird when he said we should meet at the train station last Thursday. After all, we live in the same building. But Peter said he didn't want the darkies to get any ideas. Now I know it wasn't chivalry; he didn't want anyone to see him leaving with me, both of us carrying overnight bags.

It hurts to think about the weekend in The Hague. It was so perfect. We walked all over the city holding hands. We ate in fabulous restaurants, and he paid, which was nice because I don't have much money. Peter is into cars and talks a lot about the Morgan sports car he used to have when he lived in England. One of the things he wanted to do in The Hague was go to the Louwman Museum, which is famous for old cars. We spent a morning there, and while cars are not really my thing, I have to admit the Morgan they had was pretty neat. I wish he had one here. I told him I've always wanted to see the famous painting of the girl with the pearl earrings, so on Saturday we went to the Mauritshais Museum. I spent ages just looking at that one painting while Peter went off by himself for a while. I've never seen the Mona Lisa, but I prefer this girl. She looks real, somehow. That evening at dinner, Peter gave me a pair of earrings just like the ones in the painting. I thought he was trying to tell me he loved me.

By the time we got back on Sunday evening, it was too late for dinner at the hostel, so we got take-out from a *frites* place beside the station. That's when he told me he would be moving out of the hostel the following weekend. His wife is arriving from Tasmania, and they're going to live in an apartment.

"You're married?" I cried, not wanting to believe him.

"I thought you knew," he said. He was smiling, but his eyes weren't.

"What about us?" I could hear my voice starting to wobble.

"Come on, Ellen. It was just a bit of fun for both of us. It's time to move on."

He put his arm around me but I pulled away.

"You fucker," I shouted and threw the bag of fries at him.

He just shrugged, then got on his bicycle and cycled off in the direction of the hostel.

PETER

It's never easy. They always look so wounded. Best to just walk away and forget about them.

One week later

ELLEN

I saw them at the market today—Peter and his wife. They were standing in front of the cheese stall and must have been discussing what to buy because she turned to point at something in the display case. She's smaller than me and thinner, with curly short dark hair. Peter never said anything about kids, but the two young boys standing beside them must be theirs. What a shit! It's one thing to cheat on your wife, but a whole other thing to cheat on your kids. I was going to buy some cookies at the market, but instead came straight back to my room and cried until I almost threw up.

Weekends are awful; there's absolutely nothing to do here, especially now that it's winter. Even the lab I work in is closed on weekends. As my professor explained, "We get our work done during the week so that we can spend time with family on the weekend." Yeah. Right. But what if you don't have a family? What are people like me meant to do? If I were back in Oregon, I could always find someone to hang out with. The Brits have gone back to England for the holidays, and most of the other residents have finished their courses and left. I never thought I'd say it but I miss them. I had this great idea that Peter and I would go to Paris for Christmas or New Year. Instead, I'm stuck in this miserable hostel. I can't afford to fly back to the States for the holidays, and there's nowhere in Europe I want to go, not by myself.

January

ELLEN

When I first got here, my professor suggested I sign up for a Dutch class. I couldn't see why; it isn't as if anyone else in the world speaks Dutch, and everyone I work with is fluent in English. But when Peter dumped me, I had nothing to do in the evenings, so I went to the language laboratory on campus. It's funny, but I enjoyed getting back into learning a new language. A lot of Dutch words are a mix of German and English, and it helped that I had a semester of German in college. I like being able to go into shops and hand over the correct change, not just hold out my palm with a bunch of coins in it and wait for the shop assistant to pick out the right ones.

One of the people I met at the language lab, a girl from Kuwait, asked if I would like to come along to a *koffietijd* with her. Some of the professors' wives host a coffee morning on Saturdays for foreigners to practice their Dutch. Amal said there were three people in her group, and that Anneke, their hostess, wouldn't mind if I joined in. That's where I met Julia. I recognized her immediately, and when she spoke, the Australian accent confirmed it. At first I was afraid I'd let something slip about Peter and me, but considering we were all using our limited Dutch vocabulary, I needn't have worried. As the newcomer, Anneke asked me where I was from, where I was living in Groningen, and what brought me to Holland.

When it came time to leave, Julia turned to me and said, "You must know my husband, Peter. He stayed at that hostel for a couple of months." She was smiling.

I felt a knot in my stomach.

"Yes, I've met Peter...." For a moment I didn't know what else to say, but then I rambled on about there being only four white people staying at the hostel, so inevitably we had met and gotten to know each other a little.

"Everybody else is from...you know...Africa or Samoa or Egypt or somewhere like that, and their English isn't great. The four of us used to get together sometimes and have a drink in the bar upstairs."

I smiled back at her, hoping she would accept my token of innocence.

"I'm so glad he had company there," Julia said. "We couldn't leave Tasmania until the boys finished their school term so he had to come here on his own. I've two sons—Simon's fourteen and Neville eleven. They'll be going to school here in a week or so. In at the deep end, I'm afraid, for everything is in Dutch. Still, I'm sure they'll learn something and not fall too far behind when we go home. You must come over and meet them some time."

Deep inside I was filled with desperation; despite everything, I still wanted Peter in my life.

"Yes. I'd like that very much," I lied, with perhaps a little too much enthusiasm.

JULIA

I feel smothered in this place. The Dutch are so organized and everything works perfectly; even the trains run on time. But I have nothing to do all day. Once the boys leave for school in the morning and Peter pedals off to the Institute, I find myself wondering how I'm going to fill the hours until they come home again. Because we go to the market on Saturdays—for entertainment as much as necessity—I don't need to do much grocery shopping during the week. Peter leaves me the car, but Groningen is miles from anywhere interesting. If we were in Amsterdam, things might be different; I could go to museums and galleries, wander along the canals, be a tourist. Back in Hobart I'd be sitting in my office at school, organizing the timetable for next term. It's one of the things I like least about my job, but I wish I were there right now.

Everyone at St. Mary's College was so excited for me—going to Europe for six months. If they only knew. Some days just to get out of this apartment, I walk to the city center and spend hours looking in shop windows. I know all the displays by now and how often they are changed: the dress shops, every week; the shoe shop, every fortnight; the jewelry shop, never. I'll sit for hours in a coffee shop watching women chatting to each other, eavesdropping on their conversations and trying to make out what they are talking about. The highlight of the day is when the boys come home from school. I'm amazed at how well they've adjusted. They seem happy, not missing their friends too much. They prattle on about what happened in class, not noticing that they scatter Dutch phrases amidst the English ones. Peter usually gets in just before dinner, and afterwards he helps the boys with their homework. We have a television, but all the programs are in Dutch. I watch the news, then return to my book. Fortunately, the library has a good English language collection. Otherwise, I'd probably go mad.

At least I have something to look forward to this week. I've invited the American girl I met at *koffietijd* for dinner next Friday. She seems very nice. Peter has already met her, and I'm sure the boys will like her.

PETER

There must be 150,000 people in Groningen and Julia manages to meet Ellen in her first month. They don't just meet, they become friends! She's invited Ellen for dinner on Friday. This is going to be a little awkward, to say the least. I made it clear to Julia that she should have asked me first.

"But she said she knows you, darling. From the hostel. She said you used to drink together in the pub."

I'll offer to pick Ellen up from the hostel. That way I'll have a chance to tell her to keep her mouth shut.

ELLEN

It was awkward at first being alone with Peter in the car on the way to their apartment. I wasn't sure what he would say, especially as I decided to wear the pearl earrings he gave me. He was quiet at first, but after a while he put his hand on my thigh.

"You won't say anything to Julia about us, will you?" he said.

When I didn't answer, he squeezed hard.

"I wouldn't want you to hurt her," he said, turning to look at me. He smiled and gave my cheek a gentle pat.

Just before he opened the door to the apartment, he put his finger to his lips and winked.

The rest of the evening went fairly smoothly. I avoided talking to Peter and concentrated instead on the boys, especially Simon, who, once he got over his shyness, had lots of questions about America. When I asked him about school, he said all the boys in his class are talking about the upcoming *Elfstedentocht*, a long-distance ice-skating race that's held annually on the canals, weather permitting. I told him I used to skate on the lake by my parents' house in Minnesota and promised I would teach him if I could find out where to rent skates. He blushed. He's at that awkward age.

There was only one tense moment. After dinner I offered to clear the table and began to carry a few dishes into the tiny kitchen. Peter jumped up and said he would help. As he squeezed by me in that narrow space, he deliberately rubbed his crotch against me.

"Sorry," he said, turning to look at Julia who was talking to Neville and hadn't noticed a thing.

We drove back to the hostel in silence. As he pulled into a parking stall farthest from the entrance, Peter shut off the engine and turned towards me.

"You know you're beautiful," he said, drawing me towards him and kissing me. It felt so good...to be loved again. I had missed him so much. Maybe I'd have kept going, but at that moment a car drove into the parking lot, its headlights sweeping across our faces. Instinctively we both pulled back. In that brief pause I realized he would never leave her.

"I have to go," I said, getting out of the car before he had a chance to stop me.

February

ELLEN

I feel guilty every time I go over to Julia's place, dreading the moment when she opens the door, expecting her to shout at me and tell me what a bitch I am for sleeping with her husband. I hold my breath and listen to the latch turning...then the door opens and I'm swallowed up in her wonderful smile. We have tea or sometimes a glass of wine and talk about everything under the sun. Around Christmas I found the Alexandria Quartet books in the exchange library at the hostel and spent most of the holidays curled up in bed reading. I'm in the middle of the fourth book now, and Julia is reading the third. We both agree it's fascinating how Durrell manages to tell the same love story in each book, but from a different character's perspective.

Julia told me about her first husband. All I could feel was guilt; I had been prepared to take Peter away from her. Any lingering feelings I had for him were erased at that moment and since then I've tried to avoid him. If I go to the apartment to see Julia, I make sure to leave before he gets home. She has asked me to dinner twice, but I managed to come up with an excuse each time. The Taylors are back from England so I said I had arranged to go to a movie with them. The other time I said there was a social at the hostel. It wasn't a complete lie; I went upstairs and chatted to the barman for a couple of hours—social enough. I've got back into running and go out some evenings before dinner. The Dutch are weird; they never seem to pull their drapes, so there's lots to look at in the streets around the hostel. One good thing about this town—it's very safe.

JULIA

When I first met Ellen, I wondered if Peter might have slept with her. It bothered me, but gradually I came to terms with it. By then she had become a friend, and I admit I got a certain pleasure out of watching Peter squirm when she came to the apartment. He didn't know quite how to deal with the situation.

"I don't like you spending so much time with that American girl," he said to me one evening after the boys had gone to bed.

"You see her two or three times a week at least. I don't think it's good for the boys, especially Simon. Haven't you noticed? He has a terrible crush on her." Glancing towards their bedroom door, he lowered his voice.

"I'll bet she's shagging half the darkies in the hostel."

It was such a ridiculous thing for him to say—an accusation you might expect a petulant teenager to come up with. I began to laugh but stopped abruptly when I saw that he was getting angry. I know the signs.

"She's the only friend I have in this godforsaken place," I hissed. "This sabbatical was your idea, not mine, and you're never here. What do you expect me to do? Besides, I know for a fact she's not sleeping with anyone. She'd tell me if she was. And you shouldn't call them darkies. I don't want the boys hearing that word."

I got up and left the room; that usually defuses the situation.

That was the last time he said anything about Ellen. But he made a point of being late on Wednesdays. That was the afternoon Ellen usually came over. I'm sure he checked the bike stand outside when he got home just to make sure she was gone.

May

JULIA

We make bargains in life and forever after, we work to convince ourselves of their merit. Peter is one of those bargains. I know now who the real Peter is: a selfish man, a womanizer, and a jealous husband who occasionally feels the need to remind me of my place. Still, he *is* good with the boys.

At home in Australia, he usually went to Canberra for a week each month for meetings. I never really believed him when he said he had no choice; none of his colleagues spent that much time in the capitol. I used to miss him, but as I came to know him better, I looked forward to my solitary week each month. I didn't care what he did in Canberra. If he had a mistress, so what? He'd had a vasectomy so I didn't need to worry about that at least.

Now that Ellen has gone back to America I miss her already. Besides our regular Saturday morning *koffietijd*, we saw each other at least one afternoon a week. She became a savior of sorts. Cooped up here day after day without any purpose, I began to feel invisible. At home I was a respected school principal, but here I was gradually whittled down to nothing. Then I met Ellen. I think I know why she sought out my friendship. She fell in love with

Peter too. But as we spent more time together, she and I began to share *our* lives, and Peter's presence faded. We had such fun those Wednesday afternoons together. The boys adored her too. She understood what appealed to them: shooting hoops, kicking a soccer ball around in the parking lot, skating on the canal, a plate of home-made chocolate chip cookies when they came home from school. For his first serious crush, Simon chose well.

ELLEN

Julia said not to open the present until I was on the plane. I decided to wait until halfway through the flight from Schipol to New York because it was eight hours and I only had one book to read. I recognized the label on the wrapping paper—it was from that jewelry shop on Herestraat. I used to wonder at the sign hanging over the entrance, *Schaap en Citroen,* and asked Anneke about it in faltering Dutch at one of our coffee mornings. At first she looked puzzled, but then she laughed when she realized how absurd the words Sheep Lemon sound together in English. She explained that the jewelry shop was started in the late 1800s by a merger of two families, one called Schaap (Sheep) and the other Citroen (Lemon).

The gift was a silver pendant in the shape of a globe, about three quarters of an inch in diameter, mounted on a silver arm so that it rotated. There were no continents, just an inscription in Dutch: *"Het is niet alles goud wat er blinkt."* Hmm...I knew what that meant now: All that glitters is not gold.

Buried Treasure

The two women breathed heavily as they climbed the hillside behind the farmhouse. One was carrying a shovel, the other a brown paper bag with string handles. A gust of wind erupted, bringing with it a dusting of oak leaves that added to the rich-colored carpet already blanketing the ground. Their footsteps made a satisfying crunch as they waded through the yellow and brown drifts.

"How about here?" Elizabeth said, setting down the bag with an audible sigh.

A heavy-set woman in her mid-sixties with long greying hair, she was unaccustomed to any sort of exertion and moved slowly, like a large bear. The other woman, whose name was Kate, wanted to continue to the top of the hill but knew better than to insist. She tried a different approach.

"You can see the river from the top of the hill. I'm

sure there were Indians there in the past," Kate said, pointing to a rocky outcrop a few hundred yards above them.

The grey shelf of eroded sandstone looked like the prow of a ghost ship where it emerged from the hillside. Elizabeth looked up towards the outcrop, then back at Kate. Shrugging her shoulders in a gesture of resignation, she picked up the bag and continued to climb. Five minutes later they emerged from the woods. Two hundred feet below, the Wisconsin River glinted in the sunlight, its sluggish expanse belying the swift current. A wheeze escaped from Elizabeth as she set down the bag, which made a clinking sound. Looking around the grassy clearing at the edge of the ridge, Kate chose a spot in the middle of it and began to dig.

§

The plan had been hatched by the women three weeks earlier.

"I have an unusual request," Elizabeth had said that morning when she poked her head into Kate's cubicle at the state office building where they worked.

"Of course, you can say no," she added, her body already moving forward into the cramped space. Kate looked up from her computer and smiled, wishing inwardly that the interruption might be brief.

Interpreting Kate's smile as an invitation, Elizabeth squeezed herself into the second chair and launched into her story, her voice a forced whisper so Kate had to lean forward to hear what she was saying.

"I have this friend in Arizona, Luke. He's a really good friend.... I've known him since we were in college together. He's an archeologist and very well respected; he does contract work all over North America. Well, he was left a collection of Indian artifacts—arrowheads, rugs, pots...stuff like that, by a friend of his. I suppose his friend thought he'd know what to do with the collection." She paused to catch her breath. "He contacted museums and universities and managed to get most of the items housed appropriately. But some pieces were left, arrowheads mostly. It seems that every place has a collection of arrow-heads and doesn't need or want any more."

Kate shifted slightly in her chair, mentally urging Elizabeth to get to the point.

"The thing is, Luke wants the arrowheads to end up in their rightful place. Certainly not on eBay or in some rinky-dink gift shop. Some are from the Southwest, for example, and he'll look after those. But there's a bunch from the Midwest and he sent them to me," she paused dramatically, "to bury here in Wisconsin. Luke suggested that I go to a state park or a forest or some sort of natural area where I wouldn't be disturbed. There must be plenty of places like that nearby, don't you think?"

Kate burst out laughing. The thought of Elizabeth trudging around a state park in hiking boots was farcical. As far as she knew, Elizabeth's shoes had known only pavement since she was born, and the heels had become increasingly higher as the years passed. Fortunately, Elizabeth didn't take offense, acknowledging her own ineptitude freely.

"The thing is, I don't even own a shovel, let alone know where to go. I'd probably get lost, or worse still, get arrested for damaging public property." She turned her palms upward in a gesture of resignation.

"So, I was wondering...could we bury them on your land?"

She thrust a piece of paper towards Kate.

"Here's the letter from my archeologist friend describing the artifacts and his efforts to repatriate them. It's on official letterhead and signed, just in case there are any questions."

Kate read the letter carefully. Written in authoritative academic language, the provenance of the artifacts was exactly as Elizabeth had described, and the argument for returning them to their rightful place compelling.

"He suggested that we bury coins with them," Elizabeth continued. "He even sent me some new one-cent coins; they have this year's date on them. That way if anyone finds the arrowheads in the future, they'll know that they were deliberately buried instead of just left there by..." she searched for the politically correct term, "... Native Americans who lived in this area."

Kate considered the proposal. Elizabeth was right— she had the perfect place. She and her husband Paul owned 120 acres near the Wisconsin River, their property bordering a state natural area famous for a battle that took place there in 1832, the Battle of Wisconsin Heights. A roadside historic marker described the skirmish where the Sac Indian leader, Black Hawk, and sixty of his warriors held off 700 United States militia. Although Black

Hawk won that day, the militia pursued the westward fleeing Indians, eventually slaughtering hundreds of men, women, and children when they tried to cross the Mississippi.

"Okay," Kate said, handing the letter back to Elizabeth. "Let's do it."

§

They had dug three holes in all: one near the creek that bordered Kate's property, one in the pine woods, and the final hole in the clearing at the top of the hill. Kate had placed a handful of arrowheads into each hole along with two coins, then covered them with soil and tamped down the surface so that a curious animal would not disturb it. As she emptied the last of the arrowheads, one of them caught her eye. It was larger than the others, almost four inches in length and creamy white by comparison with the grey flinty appearance of the smaller ones, none of which was more than an inch in length. At the base, which was easily two inches wide, two deep notches marked where the arrowhead would have been attached to a spear. From there, the blade tapered symmetrically to a sharp point, the surfaces smooth and the sides pitted with tiny indentations.

An overwhelming desire swept over Kate: she *wanted* the white arrowhead, as desperately as Gollum had wanted to possess the ring in Tolkien's story. For Gollum the precious object would extend his life, but Kate had no rationale.

"Isn't that an eagle?" she asked, pointing towards the sky.

Elizabeth swung around and looked upward, following the direction of Kate's finger.

"Where? I don't see it."

"Oh, you missed it. It's gone behind those trees." Kate sounded apologetic.

"It's an omen, don't you think?" whispered Elizabeth. "We must be doing the right thing."

She turned back to watch Kate, who was piling soil on top of the last of the arrowheads and coins. The white arrowhead lay snugly in Kate's pocket.

Later that afternoon, when Elizabeth had gone back to her condo in town, Kate turned the white arrowhead over in her hand, marveling at the indentations along each edge. How had they been made, she wondered? Absent-mindedly she stroked her thumb against one side of the blade, testing its sharpness. The pain came as a shock. A thin line of blood seeped from the wound, welling into a red bead that dripped onto the arrow head, contrasting sharply with the white stone. She sucked on the wound, tasting the familiar metallic flavor, then pressed her index finger against the cut. The wound continued to bleed when she released the pressure and she hunted in the bathroom cabinet for an adhesive bandage. Wrapping the Band-Aid around her now pulsing thumb, she wiped her blood from the arrowhead with a dampened tissue. Order restored, Kate placed the treasure in the bottom of her jewelry box, covering it carefully with a clean handkerchief as if it too had been injured.

§

Months passed, during which Kate forgot completely about the arrowhead. Seeing Elizabeth might have jogged her memory, but Elizabeth's division had moved into a new state office building on the other side of the city, making it inconvenient for the two women to get together for a quick lunch as they had done in the past. One evening in spring as Kate was walking along the bank of the creek that ran along the boundary of her property, she thought she heard a canoe moving through the water. The creek was popular with paddlers as it meandered through a large catchment area before emptying into the Wisconsin River five miles downstream. She paused, listening to the rhythmic swish of paddles and the sound of voices murmuring indistinctly. Turning around she waited, firmly expecting to see a canoe pull into view as it rounded the bend, yet nothing appeared. It was still early in the season and she wondered whether the paddlers might have encountered an obstacle. They must be portaging, she thought. Yet, when she walked back to find them, rounding a bend from where she could see an open stretch of water, the creek was empty. She stood still, cocking her head from side to side, but the only sound she could detect was the burble of water as it lapped against the bank. Kate dismissed the incident, putting it down to fatigue—she hadn't slept well the previous night—and promptly forgot about it.

One evening later that summer while on a walk with her husband through the pine forest on their property, Kate stopped abruptly on the path. She sniffed at the air, turning her head first to the left and then the right.

"Do you smell that?" she asked. "It smells like someone is grilling meat over an open fire."

"I don't smell a thing," Paul said as he walked past her and continued along the trail.

"Stop," she insisted. "Turn round. It's coming from that direction." She waved her hand vaguely through a ninety-degree arc. "It can't be the neighbors—their place must be a mile from here as the crow flies. Maybe someone is trespassing."

Paul stopped, turned around, and sniffed demonstratively. He shook his head.

"Nothing. Are you sure you're all right?" he said, a frown on his face.

"Should we take a look?" she asked, pointing into the woods. Buckthorn had taken over the understory since the last time the pine plantation had been thinned, creating an impenetrable tangle.

"Whoever they are, if they want to have a barbecue in there, they're welcome to it," he snorted, resuming his steady pace.

Kate followed reluctantly, turning once to look over her shoulder as if she expected to see someone step out from the woods onto the path. Quickening her pace to catch up with her husband, she soon forgot about the incident.

§

It was a glorious fall afternoon—the sort of weather that begged not to be squandered indoors.

"I think I'll go for a walk," Kate said to Paul, who was

passing through the living room on the way to his study, a mug of coffee in his hand. "Do you want to come?"

"Not now." He gestured with the mug. "I've got that deadline..."

A few minutes later she heard the regular tapping of computer keys, interrupted by a pause every so often for a sip of coffee, she presumed.

"I think I'll go up on the ridge," she said, her words directed towards the study from where she heard a grunt of acknowledgement. She shrugged, pulled on a jacket that hung by the back door, and changed into her hiking boots.

The path to the top of the hill was steep, although the ground was dry; otherwise, she might have retraced her steps to the house to get hiking poles. Ten minutes later she reached the grassy clearing that marked the beginning of the ridge. Looking up, she saw a bald eagle circling effortlessly over the river valley, its white head accentuated by a yellow curved beak. She thought back to the last time she had stood in this spot. It was exactly one year ago. Her gaze dropped to the ground, searching for some indication of where the arrowheads had been buried, but there was none. She remembered the arrowhead in her jewelry box, surprised to realize she hadn't looked at it since...since she had *acquired* it. The word "stolen" didn't sit well with her.

Leaving the clearing, she walked towards the north-west where a faded sign hanging on a barbed wire fence marked the transition to the state-owned land that bordered her property. From here the trail widened and she strolled easily along the mowed path that followed the curves of the river below. A few hundred feet along, she came across a bench that someone must have donated, for there was a small metal label on the backrest. Without her reading glasses she couldn't make out the name. Offering a silent thank you to the anonymous benefactor, she sat down, feeling surprisingly tired after the relatively brief exertion. The sky to the west had a late-fall hue, with splashes of pink and orange outlining the bare tree branches. To the east, a three-quarter moon hung in the sky. In the silence of the approaching dusk, Kate heard cries coming from farther along the ridge as if several people were running and shouting. A musket shot echoed in the valley, followed by the thwap of an arrow. The cries were coming from somewhere behind her, north of the ridge where the ground dropped off steeply in a tangle of trees and dense brush. She stood up abruptly, wondering what she should do. She hadn't brought a cell phone, hadn't considered that she would be out this late. With a pang of fear, she realized that she was on public land, the area open to hunters during bow and musket season. She turned towards home, walking quickly, then breaking into a run. The noise was all around, yet she didn't see anyone. She opened her mouth to shout a warning but before the words could form, she felt a blow directly between her shoulder blades as if someone had pierced her through to the heart. A crushing pain squeezed her chest, leaving her gasping for breath. She broke out in a cold sweat. Falling to her knees, she tried to call out but no sound came. The shadow of her kneeling body cast by the moon dissolved gradually, but for a fraction of a second before she passed out she thought she saw the outline of a spear silhouetted on the ground in front of her.

"Kate! Kate!"

Her husband's voice sounded distant and muffled, but she could feel his breath. She opened her eyes and looked into his stricken face.

"What happened? Where am I?" Her voice was barely a whisper.

"Don't talk. The EMTs will be here soon." Paul patted her hand. "It's going to be okay, I promise."

She tried to raise her head, but for some reason it felt overwhelmingly heavy. She closed her eyes, yielding to the pain that now consumed her.

"Stay with me Kate! Don't leave me now, dearest," Paul cried.

But she had passed out.

§

Her ground-floor room at the Sauk Prairie Hospital looked out on rolling fields and in the distance, the Baraboo Hills. The late afternoon sun was just hitting the tops of the trees and a band of orange and gold stretched across the horizon. Kate stared at the view absentmindedly. Paul would be here soon and she had something very important to ask him. She considered how she was going to phrase her request. Her mind wasn't as clear as she would have wished, and she hadn't the energy to tell him the whole story. Nonetheless, it was imperative that he do what she asked.

She had been lucky, or so everyone said. When she hadn't returned by dusk after her hike that day, her husband went looking for her, taking a cell phone and a flashlight as a precaution. He found her lying on the ground in the grassy clearing by the rocky outcrop at the top of the ridge. She was unconscious, her breathing shallow and erratic, but she was still alive. He called 911 and gave the dispatcher enough information to get the ambulance to the farmhouse. Paul's next call was to one of his neighbors who knew the property and could direct the EMTs to the path going up to the ridge. He spread his coat over her and sat beside her on the ground, cradling her head in his lap, stroking her cheek and all the while talking to her in reassuring tones. He heard his neighbor's truck crunching up the gravel driveway, followed by the wail of an ambulance siren. Metal doors opened and clanged shut. What seemed like an eternity but was barely ten minutes, he heard the sound of feet approaching. Three pinpricks of light appeared at the edge of the clearing, two men carrying a stretcher and a woman wearing a backpack, which she lowered to the ground beside Kate. Paul laid Kate's head gently back on the ground and stood up.

"I think she must have had a heart attack. I thought maybe she had been shot but there's no sign of blood anywhere. It's still hunting season..." His voice trailed off.

The team went about their business efficiently, strapping Kate to the stretcher while Paul and his neighbor hovered in the background, their flashlights directed onto the group. Less than an hour later, Kate was admitted to the Sauk Prairie Hospital where she had bypass surgery later that night.

"How are you feeling this evening, love?" Paul asked as he closed the door gently and stepped into Kate's room.

"Tired and sore, but not too bad, I suppose." Seeing the worry on his face she added, "The doctors say I'm doing very well...on track and all that. There's no need for you to worry. They're taking very good care of me."

Paul pulled a chair over to Kate's bedside and sat down. Her hands rested on the white sheet, the left tethered to an intravenous line, the right encumbered by a pulse oximeter. A rack of machines whirred and clicked rhythmically to the side of the bed. She reached for his hand and he slid his open palm under her fingers, careful not to disturb the oximeter.

"I need you to do something for me," she said, her voice almost a whisper. "It's important."

"Anything, my love. But there's nothing important except you getting well again."

"I want you to go to my jewelry box. It's in the top drawer of the dresser in the bedroom. In the bottom of it you'll find a handkerchief wrapped around a white arrowhead. I need you to take the arrowhead to the place where you found me last week—that grassy area at the top of the ridge—and bury it."

"But..." Paul was about to say something but she pressed her fingers into his palm.

"I need you to do this soon... it'll be too dark this evening. Tomorrow morning." She looked into his eyes. "Please...just do it for me. I'll explain later.... I'm too tired to tell you why right now. Promise me."

She laid her head back onto the pillow and closed her eyes, her pale face now peaceful and relaxed. The room was silent save for the reassuring whirr of the machines.

"I promise," he said. He slid his hand out from

under hers and got up to leave, closing the door quietly behind him.

Kate allowed her mind to wander. Next spring she would take a walk along the creek and listen for the rhythmic sound of a canoe paddle slapping the water. In summer she would walk in the pine woods, her nose alert for the faintest smell of wood smoke and grilled meat. And in the fall, she would hike up to the ridge and sit on a bench in the grassy area where she had fallen, her damaged heart paying homage to a lost tribe.

The String of Pearls

Catherine Hughes had mixed feelings about turning sixty. Unlike fifty, when she had felt almost smug about reaching the half-century mark, this birthday didn't have any particular significance. Fifty-year-olds were vibrant women in the prime of their lives, but sixty presented an ugly reminder that old age was just around the corner.

Her husband had thrown a party for her fiftieth, taking over the back room of the local pub for the evening. It had been a boisterous event, although the latter half of the evening was a bit fuzzy in Catherine's memory. A photograph of her in the local newspaper the following week said it all. With her party hat askew and her cheeks, a pair of bright pink spots that matched the smeared lipstick, she looked like a rag doll. Standing beside her was her husband, Gary, his arm thrown casually around her neck as if trying to pull her closer. On Gary's left was a younger woman, standing slightly apart from the couple and wearing an expression that conveyed forbearance. The caption correctly identified Catherine, Gary, and his secretary, who was credited with helping to organize the event. His secretary had always been good at organizing things; a year later he moved in with her in anticipation of the birth of their first child. That was in July 1996, a day etched in Catherine's memory forever. Divorce had just been legalized in Ireland and Gary wanted to be at the head of the queue.

Catherine's daughters, both of whom lived in Dublin, had suggested a sixtieth birthday party but their mother was adamant; under no circumstances was she going to endure another humiliation. Instead, the family gathered at one of her daughter's houses for a Sunday brunch. Catherine was fond of her sons-in-law and adored her three grandchildren, but by the time the meal was over she was exhausted and went home early complaining of a headache. By way of compensation, her daughters suggested a quiet lunch—just the three of them—at a popular restaurant in the city. There was a three-month waiting list for reservations, but one of her daughters "knew someone" and magically, a table was secured for two weeks later.

Catherine dressed carefully that morning, not wanting to disappoint her daughters. They were always perfectly groomed, even if it was just to go to the local supermarket. Where they had acquired their fashion sense was a mystery, although their father had always been a bit of a peacock, Catherine remembered, justifying his expensive taste in clothes by telling her that clients noticed these things. He was a salesman for a multinational dairy company and traveled abroad frequently on business.

Catherine took a final look at herself in the full-length hallway mirror. The figure looking back at her gave a tiny nod of approval. She was wearing the birthday gift her daughters had given her—a tailored three-quarter-length jacket of the softest Italian Merino wool. Eschewing her predilection for brown and black, they had chosen a shade of heather that Catherine had to agree suited her, highlighting her dyed auburn hair. This was the most expensive piece of clothing she owned, a fact she had discovered a few days earlier when she exchanged the jacket for a larger size in Dublin's premier department store.

Tilting her chin upward, Catherine made a slight adjustment to the silk scarf around her neck. That was another difference between fifty and sixty years of age, she thought wryly. At fifty her neck had still been firm and smooth, but now there was a hint of a double chin. She looked down at her shoes, a pair of well-worn black pumps that she had polished in an attempt to revive their jaded appearance. At least they match the handbag, she thought. It too was showing signs of age, but like an old friend, it had become too familiar to replace.

§

The degustation menu at Restaurant Patrick Guilbaud on Merrion Square in Dublin lived up to its two Michelin stars. Not that Catherine had any basis for comparison. She had grown up in a small town in Donegal where the only eatery was a Chinese takeout place with a dubious reputation. Dining options improved considerably when she moved to Dublin to go to university, but money was always tight. As a student she had subsisted on Irish stew, cheese on toast, and whatever her flatmates' parents donated when her friends went home for a weekend. Then came marriage and eleven months later the twins, foreclosing any dreams she might have had of dining out on a regular basis.

"The coat looks great on you, Mammy," Ciara said, when the waiter had taken their order.

"And I like what you did with the scarf," Aisling chimed in.

Catherine smiled affectionately at her daughters, of whom she was very proud. They had both followed in their father's footsteps, one a sales executive with Guinness and the other in the trade section of the Department of Foreign Affairs.

"Enough about me. Tell me what's going on in your lives," Catherine said.

Perhaps because she had recently seen them, the conversation didn't immediately turn to her grandchildren. Instead, her daughters launched into a discussion of their work issues as if they had not seen each other in months. Catherine understood; the twins never got a moment to themselves at family gatherings, being interrupted constantly by the demands of children and husbands. She found herself nodding and smiling, but not really following much of what they were saying. Fortunately, the food arrived and the topic switched to summer holiday plans, an upcoming family wedding, and finally politics—the bedrock of every Irish gathering.

After an unhurried and utterly delicious three-hour meal, she said goodbye to her daughters and began to walk back to her car, which she had parked almost a mile from the restaurant. Driving through the city center had become an exercise in futility with Ireland's booming economy. People had moved to Dublin in droves, but public transportation hadn't kept apace, forcing them to drive to work with the resultant rush hour chaos. The Celtic Tiger—the nickname for Ireland during its boom years—was at its peak; even her own daughters admitted to flying to London for weekend shopping trips.

Leaving the restaurant on Merrion Square, Catherine turned right in the direction of Trinity College. Tour buses lined Nassau Street, their passengers directed towards the entrance to the college where they would inevitably wait in long lines to view the Book of Kells. The ninth century manuscript of the four gospels housed in the Old Library—a master work of Western calligraphy—was one of the "must see" items for any tourist visiting Ireland. How things have changed, she thought. As a student at Trinity, she used to wander through the library barely glancing at the book, a page of which was turned every day to showcase its stunning beauty.

On a whim, Catherine decided to follow a group of American tourists and walk through the college. Distinguished by their sensible shoes, they came in droves year after year, pouring out of the tour coaches to take in the sights of Dublin and the rest of the country. It was great for the economy, her daughters assured her, but she was saddened by the invasion, feeling as if she and the country were losing something precious.

Catherine had mixed feelings about her four years as a student at Trinity. Looking back, those years had been the most wonderful of her life, but at the time she had felt like an imposter. She'd had a chip on her shoulder about coming from rural Donegal, the first person in her family to attend university and on a full scholarship, of course. Her fellow students exuded an aura of cultured and confident Englishness, even though most of them had grown up in Ireland. Passing by the Buttery, she remembered a particularly embarrassing occasion when one of her classmates commented on what she was wearing that day.

"Where did you find that hideosity?" the girl had said, her plummy accent emphasizing the derisory remark.

Catherine had been so proud of her "find" at the second-hand Dandelion Market, the only place she could afford to shop. That evening she threw the tie-dyed sweater into the trash and reverted to the dull, sensible knits she had brought from Donegal. During those four years, she acquired a protective shell that enabled her to thrive, but inside she carried the memory of that shameful exposé.

Leaving the campus by the main gate, Catherine turned left towards the shopping district. She hadn't given herself a birthday present, not yet at least, reasoning that she had a full year during which she could justify spending money on herself. However, that morning as she examined her reflection critically in the hallway mirror, the germ of an idea had begun to form. Walking past the bronze statue of Molly Malone at the bottom of Grafton Street, she glanced at the sculpture of the young woman whose bare neck and voluptuous breasts were being caressed by a young tourist while his friends jeered him on. Catherine took it as a presentiment; she was going to buy a string of pearls.

"All necks are improved by pearls," her grandmother used to say when asked why she always wore the same piece of jewelry, a long rope of pearls she doubled around her neck.

"And another thing. If you ever buy pearls, make sure they're real. Nobody will notice the difference, but *you* will."

When the old lady died, the pearls were left to Catherine's aunt as the eldest daughter, with Catherine's mother inheriting a pair of gold earrings, a poor consolation prize, in Catherine's estimation. For years Catherine had held out hope that Gary would buy her a string of pearls for their silver wedding anniversary, but that milestone was never achieved.

Situated on the corner of Grafton Street and Wicklow Street, Weir and Sons had been in the business of selling upmarket jewelry and watches to wealthy patrons for over a 150 years. Catherine had never been inside the store, and she opened the heavy oak door with some trepidation. Once inside, she paused for a moment to get her bearings. The interior felt opulent. It wasn't just the tall glass display cases from which ornate silver teapots reflected the light, nor the displays of timepieces with names she recognized from advertisements in glossy magazines. Rather, it was the restrained quiet of the room. She noticed several suited assistants, all of whom seemed to be busy, although only a couple of them were actually attending to clients. The deep pile carpet muffled the sound of her steps as she approached a young man behind the counter, his back to her. As if he sensed her approach by instinct, he turned and smiled.

"How can I help you, madam?" he asked, the words sounding excessively formal.

To her ear it sounded like "modom" and she almost laughed, but she reminded herself that she looked like the sort of person who shopped in Weirs regularly. It was the coat, and perhaps also the residual effects of having lunched at a Michelin-starred restaurant. She straightened her shoulders slightly and looked directly at the young man.

"I'm interested in a string of pearls."

"Of course, madam. If you would just step over here," he said, gesturing with his hand.

He moved to a display case across the showroom and Catherine followed.

"As you can see, we have a wide range."

Catherine wondered if she should place her handbag on the display case or down by her feet. She settled for the latter, afraid that the worn metal clasp might scratch the unblemished glass. Leaning over the case, she pointed to a modest string of medium-sized white pearls.

"Something like that, I think."

The assistant opened the case and removed the necklace, placing it on a dark blue velvet pad on top of the case.

"The choker. Absolutely classic. They suit every neckline. These particular pearls are some of the finest Akoya saltwater cultured pearls you can find."

Catherine read the discreet tag that hung from the clasp—€5,000. She hadn't expected to pay quite that much. Still, it *was* her birthday. As if he had read her thoughts, the assistant removed another similarly-sized string of pearls from the case and placed it on the velvet pad. Even in the artificial lighting of the store, she could see these were not as lustrous as their companion.

"These are Chinese freshwater pearls, still quite lovely, but not as exclusive the Akoya. Akoya are triple A grade." He nodded for emphasis.

Her puzzled look prompted him to continue, and for the next few minutes he gave her a lecture on pearls—how they are cultured and the qualities that distinguish them. She took the first string, examined the clasp mechanism carefully so as not fumble, and closed the pearls around her neck. It didn't seem right that the young man would help her—a gesture too intimate to endure. The pearls felt cold against her skin, as if someone had traced a line across her throat with a shard of ice. She looked at herself in the mirror, turning her neck from side to side. The collar of her coat hid the necklace from view; she unbuttoned it and let it slide off her shoulders. The string of pearls emerged from behind the Merino collar, caressing her collarbones and ending a couple of inches below the little sunken pocket at her throat. Her eyes shifted from the perfection of the pearls to the wrinkled skin at her neck. She looked into her own eyes in the mirror and recognized the expression—a mixture of sadness and regret. Unhooking the clasp, she placed the pearls back on the velvet pad.

"I'll think about it," she said as she buttoned up her

coat. She thanked the young man for his help, adding, "I've learned a lot." Bending down to retrieve her handbag, she turned and walked to the door, which closed silently but firmly behind her. The feeling of disappointment that had come over her in the store settled in her chest as she walked back to her car. She had waited too long, left it too late, she realized. It was too late to become the person who dressed impeccably, whose shoes and handbag always matched her outfit, whose husband would give her pearls and never leave.

The Conversation

"People like us, who believe in physics, know that the distinction between past, present, and future is only a stubbornly persistent illusion."

Albert Einstein

Jean paused on her way out of the apartment to scribble a telephone number in the Notes section of her desk diary. The number was the only thing she remembered of the dream she had been immersed in when her alarm went off that morning. The other details had dissipated even before she turned to her husband to deliver a perfunctory kiss, whereupon he grunted and rolled over to face the wall, his breathing settling back into a gentle purr. She tried saying the number aloud as she walked to the elevator, hoping that the recitation might trigger some recognition.

The area code was irritatingly familiar and yet she couldn't quite pin it down. East coast? West coast?

A pinging sound from the speaker in the elevator ceiling announced her arrival at the ground floor. The doorman greeted her with a cheerful, "Good morning, Dr. Bellamy." To which Jean responded with a smile and a wave of her hand.

"No cab today, Gerry. I think I'll walk," she said and stepped into the bright sunlight of the Manhattan morning.

Although it would take almost an hour, walking to the Icahn School of Medicine would allow her to organize her thoughts in anticipation of the confrontation she was going to have with her department chairman. He had hijacked her latest patent application, contributing nothing of intellectual value, yet insisting that his name should come first on the document. It was the third time he had pulled this maneuver, and she knew that unless she threatened to leave the university, he would continue to take advantage of her for the remainder of her career. It had to stop.

§

"How did it go?" her husband asked later that evening. They were seated opposite one another at the dining room table, her husband helping himself to the platter of chicken tikka masala. They rarely cooked during the week, relying instead on Deliveroo and the numerous excellent restaurants in the area. Jean pushed her plate away and banged her fists on the table, the sound resonating in the high-ceilinged room. She turned to look out the windows of their 36th floor apartment, her gaze drifting towards the East River and the United Nations Headquarters. She let out a long sigh.

"Same as always. He says that as he is a co-investigator on the grant, he should get credit for the IP, share everything, good and bad. The usual platitudes." Her voice was flat.

They looked at each other through the wisps of steam rising from the platter of curry.

"God, how I hate that man! And before you say I can quit at any time..."

She glared at her husband.

"Well, that's what you were going to say, isn't it? It's what you always say: just walk away. Well, I don't want to walk away. I like what I do and I'm good at it. It's important work."

Her voice had risen to a shout. Tears of frustration began to well up in her eyes, and she brushed them away with her sleeve. Her husband got up slowly, came around to her side of the table, and placed his hands gently on her slumped shoulders. They sighed in unison. This conversation was excruciatingly familiar, repeated every few months for the past nine years, ever since he had sold his business for several million dollars. Accustomed to money all of his life, the rich New York lifestyle suited him. For Jean, money hardly mattered unless it was a major grant from the National Institutes of Health to fund her laboratory. Research was her life. It defined her, validated her, and gave her an indisputable authority amongst her husband's Wall Street friends. He might have made a fortune, but *she* was a tenured Professor at Mount Sinai doing cutting edge molecular biology research. As far as she was concerned, they were equals.

Born in England and educated at Cambridge, she had emigrated to the United States in her early twenties to do postdoctoral research at the University of Wisconsin in Madison. She was forty-three when she met David, a man fifteen years her senior. Under normal circumstances she would have dismissed the liaison as ill-advised, but her father's death the previous year had been a wake-up call that there was no longer anyone in the world who put her first. David, divorced and with two financially-independent adult children, was swept off his feet by this spirited and determined scientist. He pursued her patiently, finally persuading her to move from San Diego to New York where Mount Sinai was delighted to accommodate her well-funded research laboratory.

"Let's go to the cottage this weekend. What do you think?" David said, squeezing her shoulders encouragingly.

"You go ahead," she said in a tired voice. "I have a lot of work to do."

After the sale of his company, she and David had spent some months looking for the perfect weekend hideaway. While he would have preferred a property on Long Island, she pointed out that she needed to be able to get back to her laboratory at short notice. So, they settled on an old farm house in the Hudson River Valley near New Paltz, transforming a ramshackle ruin into a charming cottage.

§

The research wing of Mount Sinai was quiet when she went to work the following day, a Saturday. She punched in the key code to her laboratory, noting that no lights were on in the suite of connected rooms. Just like her chairman, who was accustomed to saying "They don't pay me for overtime," her graduate students took their weekends seriously and rarely came in to work. She smiled as she remembered a professor she had known in Madison who insisted that Saturdays were the best day of the week to do experiments.

"Ye don't need a hypothesis on Saturdays," he used to say in his Northern English accent, chuckling mischievously. "Ye just try anything, and have a bit o' fun!"

Many years later she had watched his Nobel acceptance speech. High above the podium where a page from one of his lab notebooks was projected onto a large screen, he had pointed to the date at the top of the page.

"See? It was a Saturday...the day it all started! And look where it took me," he cooed triumphantly.

As a fellow countryman, he had gone out of his way to be kind to her during her first few months in America. It was from him she learned that scientific research in the United States was more of a business than an avocation, and to be successful you had to approach it with the mindset of a company director. His mentorship had been critical in her professional development, and he would have been delighted to see her coming to work in her laboratory on a Saturday.

It came to her in a flash. The telephone number she had scribbled down the previous day was her old telephone number from when she lived in Madison. How could she have forgotten? All the same, that was thirty-five years ago and there had been many telephone numbers in the interim. She put the thought aside and began to get organized for the task at hand, changing the medium in an incubator full of cell cultures. Normally, this would be done by a graduate student, but she insisted on taking her turn, knowing that it conveyed a strong message that she was deeply invested in their research projects.

Later, she sat down at her desk with a cup of coffee and opened a manuscript she was reviewing. The authors were from the University of Wisconsin, and for a few minutes she allowed her thoughts to wander back to Madison. An image of her first apartment came to mind. She had rented it because it came fully furnished and was on a bus line, not realizing that the neighborhood was somewhat seedy. Within a few days of her moving in, two undercover police officers knocked on her door and asked if they could have a word with her. A man had been found dead in the apartment across the hallway and they suspected foul play. Soon afterwards she read in the state newspaper that a local woman had been arrested for the man's murder. Within a few months she found another place to live, a tiny cabin on the north shore of Lake Mendota, in Middleton.

On a whim, she grabbed the telephone on her desk and punched in the Middleton number, expecting to hear a disembodied voice informing her it was no longer in service. Instead, the phone was answered on the fourth ring.

"Hello?" The voice was female.

Momentarily taken aback, Jean stammered, "Who... who am I speaking to?"

"Jean Bellamy."

As if it had come alive in her hand, she jammed the phone back into its cradle. Her mind raced as she tried to make sense of what she just heard. She had dialed her own telephone number from thirty-five years ago, and the woman who answered had said her name was Jean Bellamy. Perhaps the woman had seen that name on her caller ID and read it aloud instead of saying her own name? That must be it, Jean thought, feeling a little foolish. For a moment she had jumped to a very different conclusion. She resumed her manuscript review and was soon engrossed. By the time she left the lab that evening, she had forgotten about the incident.

It was several days later when a casual scan of her desk diary on her way out of the apartment reminded her of the telephone number and the strange call, and she puzzled over it as she walked to work. She was sure the woman had a slight English accent, detectable in the way she said "Hello," dropping the final rounded vowel. By the time Jean got to her office she had resolved to call the number again. After that she could put the matter to rest. She texted her husband to say she would be late and waited until the early evening to make the call. This time the phone was picked up promptly.

"Hello. This is Jean," a voice said.

"Am I speaking to Jean Bellamy?" Jean asked, this time with more authority in her voice.

"Yes. I'm Jean," came the response. "How can I help you?" The accent was definitely English.

"Are you in Madison, Wisconsin by any chance?" Jean asked, trying not to sound like a telemarketer.

"Well, actually I'm in Middleton, but I work in Madison—at the university."

"You sound like you're from England," Jean said. "Were you born there?"

"Yes, I was. I've lived there all my life...until a few months ago, that is. Is my accent that obvious? I thought I was beginning to sound like an American." This was followed by a laugh.

Jean took a deep breath.

"Actually, *my* name is Jean Bellamy too, and I was born in England."

"Really? Where abouts?"

Jean found herself at a loss for words. She needed time to think.

"Hello...hello...are you still there?"

An image leapt into Jean's mind of a young girl, leaning against a window frame in the kitchen of a tiny cabin, curling a white telephone cord around her fingers as she looked out towards a lake.

"It was nice talking to you," Jean said abruptly, and replaced the handset in its cradle.

For several minutes she stared at the phone, her mind struggling to come to terms with what had just happened. She was a scientist, she reminded herself; there had to be a logical explanation. If there was a Jean Bellamy at the University of Wisconsin, a Google search should be able to locate her. For the next hour she scoured the university website, paging through lists of faculty, staff, and students, but she came up with nothing. Nor could she find any information on Facebook or LinkedIn about a Jean Bellamy in Madison or Middleton. The only relevant hit was a manuscript she had published while she was a postdoc at the university.

Having eliminated all logical explanations, she was left with something utterly improbable. Could there be such a thing as a parallel universe, she wondered? The idea wasn't new. Every so often there would be an article in *Scientific American* or *New Scientist* that referenced String Theory and a metaverse of alternate worlds. She reminded herself that just because she didn't understand how something worked didn't mean it wasn't true. After all, she didn't understand dowsing, yet had seen a friend find a buried water pipe with a bent clothes hanger. She typed in "String Theory and Parallel Universe" on her keyboard and spent the next hour reading about the multiverse, which, by all accounts had some noteworthy proponents. The notion of being able to communicate with one's younger self, with all of its potential ramifications, was earth shaking. But that raised a critical question: what would you tell that younger self?

The question dogged her as she walked home that evening. It reared its head again during the small hours of the night and was still there the following morning.

"You seem a little distracted," her husband remarked over breakfast.

"I didn't sleep well," she admitted. "I'm trying to sort out something.... It's complex."

"Science?" he asked. She nodded.

He smiled at her. "You'll get there. You always do."

Jean was accustomed to advising her graduate

students and postdocs, but this was different. The person on the other end of the telephone line was herself; if she did offer advice, what would it be? And would it alter the girl's life, *her* life? The idea was terrifying. She listened as the debate played back and forth in her head.

"Why would you give advice?" a voice asked.

"To win, of course," came the answer.

"What's a win?"

The question surprised her. Tentatively she allowed her mind to explore some options: a Nobel Prize, winning the lottery, becoming rich and famous.... She struggled to find some prize, some achievement that would merit turning the clock backwards.

"Haven't you already won?" the voice insisted. "What would you change about the last thirty-five years if you had the chance?"

For the next few days Jean wrestled with the key question: what would she change? But with each flight of fancy, each alternative life, her scientific brain forced her to examine the consequences. At any moment in those thirty-five years she might have wished her life to be otherwise, but now she could appreciate its extraordinary richness.

§

"I think I'll drive up to the cottage for a couple of days," she said to her husband that evening. "We don't have any social engagements, do we?"

He glanced at the calendar hanging on the wall beside the refrigerator.

"No. Nothing until the weekend. You'll be back Friday, then?"

"Yes. Friday."

The drive from Manhattan to New Paltz took a little under two hours. Traffic was light on the interstate at that time of day, although it took her another half an hour to drive through the town itself. In summer New Paltz burst at the seams, with students taking classes at the university and holiday makers drawn to the hiking and biking opportunities at the nearby Mohonk Preserve. Bistros and Brew Pubs lined the streets, their young patrons spilling out onto sidewalk seating. As she waited for the traffic lights to change at the end of Main Street, she examined the parade of pedestrians; everyone looked to be in their 20s, radiating energy, and smiling and laughing at the pure pleasure of life.

The cottage sat in a grove of beech trees, hidden from the winding road that continued uphill to the Mohonk Preserve with its iconic Mountain House Hotel. She and her husband had stayed at the hotel several times when they were house-hunting in the area and had become lifetime members of the Preserve, free to wander its miles of carriage trails. Jean loved spending time here, and although she would never admit it to her husband, she preferred coming by herself. Perhaps her husband felt the same way too, for they seemed to orchestrate their visits when one of them had a commitment in the city. She made a pot of tea and sat on the deck that overlooked a sweep of fields and woods stretching to the south and east towards the Hudson River. She didn't want to think about the phone call just yet and allowed her mind to drift. The steady hum of insects, interrupted occasionally by a bird's chirping, lulled her into a state of contentment, and she found herself thinking: what more could anyone desire?

The screech of a blue jay interrupted her reverie and reminded her that she had a purpose in coming to the cottage. The Manhattan apartment, though spacious, didn't have an attic or basement, and as a result all of her old papers and memorabilia were here. Half an hour later she emerged from the damp-smelling basement carrying a plastic storage box that she brought around the side of the house and deposited on the deck. Settling herself comfortably, she took three thick notebooks out of the box—her diaries from when she lived in Wisconsin.

She outlined the problem in her mind. The key was how to persuade her younger self that she, Jean Bellamy, aged sixty and living in Manhattan, was real. It would be a hard sell. One approach might be to describe what was going on in the girl's life at that moment. How else could Jean know those details unless she had been there? But the girl might argue that anyone could know where she lived and worked. What if she could convince the girl that she was able to predict the future? Tell her what was going to happen the following day or week. Perhaps then the girl would listen. Jean still wasn't sure what advice she would offer, but the challenge filled her with excitement.

The first diary entry was a vivid description of Jean's first day in America. She had just completed her dissertation at Oxford and with the optimism of youth, was apprehensive yet confident that she would thrive in her new lab. Jean read quickly, skimming the pages with their familiar names, places, and events. She found herself smiling at the freshness of the descriptions and how thoroughly her younger self had invested in this new life. Sometimes a description was at odds with what she remembered, forcing her to consider the imperfection of memory. After all, it was just synapses and neurochemicals that captured those stories, and like all molecules they turned over on a regular basis.

She flipped through the pages quickly until she came to today's date, curious to see what was happening in her life all those years ago. Perhaps she could pick an event a few days hence and describe it in detail to the girl during their next conversation. There would naturally be some incredulity when Jean suggested that they were one and the same person, just living in parallel strands of time. She rehearsed what she was planning to say, listening to the words and the inflection in her voice.

"Look," she would say, "I know pretty much every-thing about your life right now. I know you live by yourself in a cabin overlooking Lake Mendota. Your landlady is called Edith and there's a Native American bird mound in your back yard. This weekend you plan to go to Devil's Lake with a guy called Ralph. He works in the lab opposite yours, and he's offered to teach you how to rock climb."

Jean found that she didn't need to read the next few pages of the diary. Even now she could remember that first "date," the hike up to the East Bluffs at Devils Lake State Park, the thrill of his nearness when he tied the climbing harness around her waist, her desperation to please. His soon-to-be-divorced wife didn't like rock climbing, which was his passion in life, together with science. But Jean was determined to love the sport—his sport—and love him too. She had succeeded at both, and within a few months he moved into her cabin on the lake. Over the next two years she wrapped herself in his life, catering to his every whim, always putting his wants and needs first. Looking back on it now, she admitted to herself that they had some wonderful times together. They rock climbed all over the country—Yosemite, Red Rocks, Devil's Tower, Black Canyon of the Gunnison, the Shawangunks. They were the perfect couple, and she had been certain they would get married when his divorce was finalized. Instead, he packed his things and moved out. He told her he couldn't explain why, that she deserved someone better. Then he moved in with a friend of hers.

The sun was low in the sky when she closed the final diary. She had poured her heart and soul into those notebooks, and being reminded of that anguished time was painful. What could she possibly say to her younger self that would make life any easier now, or better in the future? She wanted to get it right—there would only be one chance.

What would you like to know about your future? With a heavy heart Jean realized that the girl would have only one question. She would ask if Ralph was going to fall in love with her. Nothing profound, nothing worthy. The whole idea of calling her was futile.

Jean got up stiffly, carried the box into the living room, and closed the French doors. Pouring herself a glass of wine, she sat on a sofa in the dimly-lit room, allowing her mind to empty. It felt as if she had been on a long journey but was now finally home. A book of poems by Mary Oliver lay on the coffee table. Picking it up, she opened it at random and read.

The past is the past and the present is what your life is,
And you are capable of choosing what that will be.
Put your lips to the world, and live your life.

A thought struck her and she switched on a lamp, the narrow pool of light warming her. Retrieving the first of the diaries from the box, she riffled through its pages, this time going backwards from the date where she had started hours earlier. With a tiny feeling of satisfaction, she read: "Got a strange phone call today. The woman said her name was Jean Bellamy, and she was born in England. She didn't say where. She sounded American."

A Kindness

The face on the computer screen wobbled for a moment and Margaret wondered whether her mother might be having a stroke. There was a wobble in her mother's voice too, but within a few seconds the mouth and words became synchronized. This mismatch happened frequently during their computer conversations, and each time it prompted a tiny jolt of fear in Margaret's chest. Her mother was eighty-seven with brain and body showing inevitable signs of wear. Margaret dreaded the finale.

It hadn't been easy to convince her mother to use an iPad for their weekly chats, but once she moved to the retirement home and heard from other residents that calling America was free, she adapted quickly. International telephone calls were prohibitively expensive in Ireland in the old days, she reminded Margaret, and she had insisted on rationing them just as she had with food during the war. These days, at precisely 3:30 every Sunday afternoon, Margaret's mother stabbed at the familiar icon on her tablet until her daughter's face appeared, then launched into conversation as if Margaret were sitting across from her at the kitchen table in the old house in the west of Ireland. Their relationship, always taut, had improved considerably in the past year. No longer responsible for the upkeep of a deteriorating house, her mother had relaxed into a life where meals were served, her room was cleaned regularly, and someone else changed the sheets. Her mother still held the reins firmly when it came to provoking guilt during these weekly conversations, but as Margaret was paying her mother's bills, the impact of these tiny jabs was blunted.

"I was chatting with Monica Collins after mass yesterday," her mother said in a tone that suggested *news*, the currency of her diminished life.

Margaret tried to conjure an image of her childhood neighbor but could only manage a generic female shape wearing a headscarf tied tightly under the chin. The church was easier to picture. Mass at St. Ignatius had been a weekly ritual until Margaret went to nursing school in England and no longer felt the need to pretend.

"She said Geraldine Tormey had died." A dramatic pause was followed by, "Didn't she do nursing with you in Liverpool?"

Without giving Margaret a chance to answer, her mother continued.

"It was cancer. Went to her brain in the end. It took her..."

Margaret interrupted and noticed a frown appearing

on her mother's forehead, accompanied by a tightening in the corners of her mouth.

"Did she have any family?" Margaret asked.

"Two sons, according to Monica, with families of their own now. She didn't say how many grandchildren, but everyone was there at the end, thank God. It's the sort of death anyone would want."

She heard the reproach in her mother's voice but ignored it.

"And her husband? Didn't he..." Margaret's voice trailed off. She didn't know what it was she wanted to ask about Geraldine's husband.

"He's devastated, according to Monica, but he's had time to adjust. Seems she's been going downhill for a year or more. Monica said he was devoted to her. Looked after her day and night, right up to the end."

Another little jab, but Margaret decided to let it pass. There was a time when she would have defended her decision to take a job in Denver, enumerating for her mother all the positive aspects of life in America. Now she no longer tried.

Her mother's face blurred slightly as she shook it from side to side, tut-tutting audibly.

"You used to be such good friends. Whatever happened?"

"She moved to Norway. Remember?"

"You visited her there once, didn't you?"

Taken aback at her mother remembering, Margaret paused for a moment before answering. She didn't want to continue talking about Geraldine.

"Your memory is getting better, Mammy. They must be looking after you well."

"Well enough, although I had to complain to Matron the other day. There's a new young one working here and she's useless. She forgot my cocoa, and when she finally brought it, it was stone cold."

"I'm sure she'll improve when she gets the hang of the place. Where's she from?" Margaret tried to sound conciliatory and at the same time to deflect the topic. She dreaded the possibility her mother would insist she write to the Matron. This had happened once already.

Fortunately, with her news delivered, Margaret's mother switched to familiar topics—the weather and who had visited her during the week. Margaret in turn shared what little news she had, knowing that her mother had long ago lost interest in her daughter's life. She still enjoyed hearing about her grandchildren, but they were both away in college—one in California and the other in Georgia. Neither of Margaret's daughters seemed to feel it a burden to call their mother, and she was accustomed to being interrupted at any hour of the day by the unique chimes she had entered into her cell phone. Her younger daughter was taking the MCAT exam the following week, and Margaret spent a few minutes explaining to her mother the significance of the exam when it came to applying to medical school. Margaret saw her mother's head shift slightly, the eyes glancing upward towards a clock hanging on the wall in her room—the same clock that had hung in the kitchen of Margaret's childhood home, its thick black numbers dictating the pulse of her life for eighteen years.

"Look at the time!" her mother said. "I've got to go. My bridge group will be arriving in a few minutes. I'll talk to you next week. Say hello to David for me, and tell that daughter of yours I'll be storming heaven for her exams. Bye now. Bye. Bye. Bye..."

The screen went blank and Margaret closed her laptop with a sigh, her duty done for another week.

§

Margaret woke in the middle of the night and lay quietly for several minutes as the shreds of a dream dissolved even as she tried to reconstruct it. Geraldine Tormey had been in her dream. She tried to fall back to sleep but found herself unable to stop thinking about Geraldine, almost her own age and now dead.

After an hour of unproductive mind- and breath-management she gave up. Careful not to disturb her husband, she crept downstairs, made a cup of mint tea, and carried it outside to the deck at the back of their ranch house west of Denver. The air had cooled, and the Colorado night sky was clear with just a hint of light silhouetting the mountains. She stepped inside to retrieve a throw and returned to the wicker chair on the deck, settling into the cushions and wrapping the blanket around her; she tucked her bare feet under its edge. Geraldine. An image of a tall, lean young woman in a nurse's uniform with a mop of unruly black curls corralled under a white cap brought a smile to Margaret's face.

She and Geraldine had grown up in the same town in the west of Ireland, and despite being two years apart had become close friends while at nursing school in England. When Geraldine graduated, she took a position at a hospital in the north of England. Margaret visited her once, taking the train from Liverpool to Newcastle upon Tyne. That's when she met Geraldine's boyfriend, Aksel, who lived in Norway and had spent the previous summer as a student teacher in England. Every month he would catch the overnight ferry from Bergen to Newcastle to spend a weekend with Geraldine.

Margaret tried to recall the details of that first meeting. Aksel was shorter than Geraldine, she remembered, and didn't say much; whether his English was limited or he was just shy wasn't clear to her. She liked him immediately; he had none of the swagger she was accustomed to in Irish men. They had played tennis, and despite Margaret being paired with Geraldine, he had beaten the two of them soundly. Yet he didn't gloat. Within a year the couple were married and Geraldine had moved to a small town south of Trondheim where Aksel was a school teacher.

Margaret approached the next memory, unfolding it slowly, careful not to tear its brittle wrapping. How many years ago had it happened? She had just finished nursing school and was about to start a job at the Mater Hospital in Dublin. Forty years. The boy she was dating—his name came back to her instantly, Jimmy Keenan—had just broken up with her, shattering her dreams.

The day she told her parents she was going to postpone the nursing job and hitchhike around Scandinavia instead was etched into her memory. Hoping her parents would be reassured by details, she outlined her itinerary, beginning with a ferry from Belfast to Scotland, hitchhiking across England, and another ferry to Norway. From there she would go to Oslo, then Stockholm, and finally retrace her steps to Dublin. She didn't mention Finland, although crossing the Arctic Circle was a key part of her plan.

"I'll drop in on Geraldine when I'm in Norway," she reassured them.

They were appalled. She had a good job waiting for her—how could she be so irresponsible? For the next several hours they tried to dissuade her using every argument, threat, and promise they could muster. Finally, she had stormed out of the house and caught the next train back to Dublin. In her mind the logic of her plan was unassailable. Her adventure would prove to Jimmy he had made a mistake, and he would come back to her. She had been wrong, of course.

Forty years later, she could still remember setting out on the trip. She had taken a bus to the outskirts of Dublin and, sick with apprehension, raised her thumb inexpertly. Within a few minutes a truck slowed to a stop. Running awkwardly towards the vehicle, she hoisted her backpack up into the cab and climbed inside. That first driver had been friendly and kind, and there were many more like him. Occasionally, she encountered a salacious look, a groping hand, even a blunt proposition, but she learned gradually how best to avoid these situations, if necessary, resorting to shouts and tears. Three weeks later, bristling with achievement, she mailed a postcard to Jimmy Keenan. The card showed a black and white outline of Finland with Rovaniemi, the capitol of Lapland, represented by a large red dot. Below Rovaniemi, a curved line with the magical coordinates of 66° 32' 35" stretched from Sweden to Russia. After much thought, she decided on a simple greeting: Look where I've fetched up! Love, Mags.

Margaret stifled a laugh as she reflected on her adolescent ruse. Do kids still do this sort of thing today, she wondered? She had called Geraldine from a public phone in the youth hostel in Rovaniemi. With luck, her friend would be at home, but if not, Margaret had become friendly with a young Dutch traveler in the hostel. He was heading towards Stockholm and had suggested they travel together. He would get rides more easily with a female companion, he explained, and with a male companion she would not have to worry about her safety.

The phone was picked up, and Margaret heard Geraldine's voice saying something in Norwegian.

"Geraldine, it's Mags!", she shouted into the receiver, her excitement echoing in the cramped telephone kiosk.

"Mags! Where the hell are you? I've been waiting for you to call for weeks now."

There was a new Nordic lilt in Geraldine's voice, but underneath it Margaret could still hear the west of Ireland accent. The friends chatted briefly about where Margaret was calling from and how many days it would take her to hitchhike from Rovaniemi to Trondheim, a thousand kilometers at least.

"You could always take a train or a bus," Geraldine offered.

"For heaven's sake, if I can hitchhike from Dublin to the Arctic Circle, I can get to your place," Margaret re-assured her.

Tracing the route on her map of Scandinavia, she realized that she would be able to travel with her new Dutch friend as far as Umeå, approximately four hundred kilometers to the south in Sweden, before striking out on her own to the west, across the Scandinavian peninsula to Norway.

§

The house was several miles south of Trondheim, on a small road off the main north-south highway. Margaret walked the last few kilometers as not a single car passed her once she had left the main road. Searching for a building that matched Geraldine's description—a small single-story house with a green tin roof on the right-hand side of the road—she finally saw it. Sliding her pack off, she sat by the gate and waited for her friends to come home.

They greeted her warmly, and soon they were sitting around the kitchen table, sharing the bottle of wine that she had brought, catching up on the past three years. Aksel volunteered to prepare dinner so that Margaret could spend a little time alone with Geraldine. They carried their glasses to the living room and set them down on the coffee table.

"Let me show you around the house," Geraldine said. "It's small but cozy, especially in winter. Not like that dump I had in Newcastle. Do you remember it? It was freezing all the time."

They both laughed as Geraldine led the way down a narrow hallway with three doors. She pointed to one of them.

"That's the main bathroom. You have it all to your-self—we've got an en suite."

She opened another door and stepped back to allow Margaret to enter.

"This is where you'll be sleeping," she said.

Margaret looked around, taking in the single bed with its childish counterpane. A crib had been pushed against one wall. She was about to congratulate Geraldine when she noticed the tears welling up in her friend's eyes.

"I miscarried," Geraldine said wiping the tears from her cheek with the back of her hand. "It happened two months ago so I'm still a little…"

"I am so sorry," Margaret said. "It must have been awful."

Geraldine sniffed back tears, straightened her shoulders, and took a deep breath.

"Yes. Well…there's nothing wrong with me, or so my doctor says. So we'll just try again."

Despite her positive words, Geraldine looked strick-en. Margaret stepped back into the corridor, closing the door behind her. She followed Geraldine back to the living room, wondering if she had made a mistake in coming here.

The house was silent when Margaret woke the fol-lowing morning. She found a note propped up against a container of muesli on the kitchen counter telling her to help herself to breakfast. The previous evening she had allowed herself to be persuaded to stay another night. Having the house to herself for a whole day and not having to brace herself for yet another encounter with a complete stranger on the road was seductive, especially after another few glasses of wine. Besides, the grand adventure was beginning to lose its luster. It was time to go home. But today was hers to while away the hours. She'd take a long shower, perhaps go for a walk, or maybe just sit around and read a book. She'd noticed a washer and drier in the mudroom off the kitchen the previous evening, a reminder that she had run out of clean clothes. At the end of the day her hosts would return, share more wine and laughter over another good meal, and she would go to bed ready to face the final leg of her journey.

She was alone in the living room when Aksel and Geraldine appeared in the doorway from the kitchen where they had been clearing up after dinner. Aksel touched Geraldine's arm gently as if urging her to speak.

"We've got something to ask you," Geraldine said, looking from her husband to Margaret.

"Yeah?" Margaret looked up from the magazine she was reading.

"Aksel would like to sleep with you."

Geraldine went on to explain that Aksel had never been with another woman. He found Margaret very attractive. It would be just for tonight.

Still standing together in the doorway, the couple looked at her expectantly.

The request had come out of nowhere like a bolt of lightning, and looking back now, Margaret couldn't remember how she had responded. She must have said something, she thought, or perhaps just nodded her assent. Whatever she had said or done all those years ago, she had indeed agreed.

For the next half an hour they had tried to sustain a

conversation, but eventually it dwindled. Geraldine stood up first and with an affectionate look towards Aksel, left the room, closing the door behind her. Aksel came to sit beside Margaret on the couch. She turned to face him, and he took her hand in his. Not sure what to do next, she kissed him on the lips. A few minutes later he led her from the living room, past the master bedroom, to the tiny guest bedroom where she had been sleeping. They made love in the single bed with its childish counterpane. Afterwards they lay together, neither of them speaking.

"I should go back to Geraldine. She will be feeling lonely," Aksel finally whispered.

He kissed her once more, this time on the cheek, then left. Her eyes tightly shut, Margaret listened as her bedroom door closed and another opened.

To her relief the house was silent when she woke the following morning. She ate a bowl of cereal, then wondered whether she should leave a thank-you note. Deciding against it, she closed the front door behind her, hoisted her backpack on her shoulders, and walked to the main road. Turning south towards Bergen, she put out her thumb.

§

Their friendship had not survived. Margaret told herself it was because she left Ireland soon afterwards and lost touch with many of her old friends, but it was more than that. She had wanted to put the encounter behind her. What happened had made her feel uncomfortable in a way she found impossible to articulate. Now, as she dissected the memory of that evening, she wondered why each of them had allowed it to happen? Was Geraldine trying to give something to her husband to atone for losing their baby—a kindness of sorts? And what of Aksel? Maybe his part in it was merely curiosity. As for her own motives, even now she wasn't sure. Perhaps for her too it had been a gesture of kindness. She mulled over this possibility for several minutes with a growing sense of acceptance. Kindness was a good word.

The Colorado sky was beginning to lighten with stars fading gradually. Just like memories, she thought. Reassembling this final memory of Geraldine, she laid her friend to rest.

The Business of Science

The numbers said it all. Only two of the six rats in her experiment had performed the way she hoped—hypothesized. This was science, after all. You *had* to have a hypothesis, otherwise nobody took you seriously. She pushed her hair back from her face and peered at the spreadsheet on the computer screen, checking the numbers one more time. Last week there were only three responders, three out of six female rats who did what they were supposed to—supported the hypothesis. If this continued, she'd be forced to abandon the project, *her* project. Insecurity wormed its way back into her consciousness. It was always there but she had managed to keep it under control for some time now, presenting a façade of competence. These latest results threatened to shatter that.

The last six months had been a joyous roller coaster for Anna. She had taken a postdoctoral fellowship at the University of Florida in a research group that studied olfaction. Smell was fascinating. The earliest of the senses to emerge in evolutionary terms, it was still the least well understood, even though every species relied on smell for survival. By comparison with dogs or even rats, the human ability to detect and discriminate odors was pitiful. Nevertheless, humans had always capitalized on olfaction, either disguising odors they deemed unpleasant with perfumes and air fresheners, or amplifying others they deemed valuable such as wine and blended whiskeys. If scientists understood how smell worked at the cellular and molecular level, she thought, it could be manipulated. This project was her golden opportunity if only she could make it work.

"Call me Don. Don the Don," her boss had said in his best Al Pacino Mafia voice on her first morning in the lab. He was a professor at the University's Medical School, overseeing a medium-sized research group comprising a technician, two other postdocs, three graduate students, and a handful of undergrads. Initially, he had given her a relatively straightforward project—bread and butter, he had called it. But there was a clear expectation that she would develop her own research project.

"No pressure, but you should have enough preliminary data to submit a grant application in, say, six to nine months," Don had said, leaving little doubt that she would need to get up to speed quickly.

One of the new requirements of the National Institutes of Health was that female subjects be included in all studies funded by the agency. In the past the animal equivalent of an eighteen-year-old, white male had been the gold standard, but drug companies were beginning to understand that this group represented only a fraction of the population, and that drugs could be tailored, and marketed, to many different groups: children, elderly, female, Black. Don had complied, but grudgingly. It wasn't the money—his grant budget had been adjusted generously. The problem was working with female rats.

"Females are a bloody nuisance," he told the lab group. "It would be fine if it was one female for one male, but since female rats ovulate every four to five days, it's a nightmare. Can you imagine what it would be like if women ovulated every four days? Life would be hell."

In experiments with human subjects, females were usually tested twice in their menstrual cycle, at fourteen and twenty-eight days, but with rats the mid-point and the end was less clear. Don had taken a cavalier approach, housing his female rats together in a separate room in the animal-care facility with the assumption that their individual cycles would synchronize.

"It worked in the university dorms when I was a student," he had said with a shrug that left little doubt he had taken advantage of the phenomenon.

By pure chance, Anna made a discovery in her first month in the lab that was potentially a game-changer. During a brief window in their estrus cycle, a mere six hours the morning of the first day, something strange came over female rats. Their ability to smell was boosted more than fifty-fold by comparison with male rats. It was as if they had developed super powers. If she could just work out the underlying mechanism, Anna was certain this line of research would lead to publications in high-impact journals, independent funding, and ultimately, a coveted faculty position.

Over the next few months she gathered more data until she was absolutely sure of her finding. Then, with butterflies in her stomach, she presented her data to Don and the group at their weekly lab meeting. With the aid of numerous graphs and histograms, she tried to persuade them there was something unique about these "super sniffers," as she affectionately referred to them. Initially there was skepticism, especially from Tracy, the other female postdoc in the lab, who said that somebody would have already discovered it if it were real. Anna had little patience for Tracy, who she thought was narrow-minded in her approach to science, if not downright stupid at times.

"But nobody ever looks this closely at female rats," Anna insisted. "Nobody bothers to test them during this time in their cycle. After all, it's barely six hours. People always focus on the middle and the end, like humans."

Her voice rose in exasperation. If she couldn't persuade her own lab group, how was she ever going to assert her independence as a scientist? Dedication and hard work were not enough; you had to have self-confidence and argue your position persuasively.

Don's curiosity was piqued, especially when he saw the raw data.

"Who'd have thought females were that sensitive?" he said, with a knowing look directed at Hong Jin and Steve, the only other males in the group. Hong Jin kept his eyes fixed on his hands. His comprehension of English might not be great, Anna thought, but at least he understood the rudiments of *#MeToo.* Steve gave a coarse laugh. As an undergrad in Don's empire, he understood his role—to be a sycophant and wash glassware.

"I think you might be on to something," Don continued in an upbeat voice. "Maybe you should think of presenting at the Society for Neuroscience meeting this year. Write an abstract. Stake your claim to the idea. Between now and then you'll be able to run a few more experiments and tidy up the statistics. I'm not sure what you're going to say about relevance, though. I mean, it's not as if the TSA is going to walk around an airport with drug-sniffing rats on a leash..." He burst into peals of laughter and was quickly joined by Steve.

"You are so funny, Don," Tracy giggled, her body quivering with delight.

The following week Anna's nightmare began. At first it was only one out of six female rats that failed to detect the dilute-odor stimulus in the sniff test. She put it down to chance; the impact of the result on her statistics would be negligible. But five days later when she tested the same animals, three out of six failed to respond, then four out of six. At their next lab meeting, Anna admitted to the group that things were not going so well.

"Maybe it's something to do with the season, or the phase of the moon," Tracy suggested.

Anna didn't know whether Tracy was joking or serious. All the same, it had been spring when Anna first began her experiments, but now the summer heat and humidity had arrived with a vengeance. Maybe there was something to Tracy's suggestion.

"And what about the construction that's going on?" Tracy continued. "There's been a lot of hammering at that end of the building. It could be upsetting the rats, messing with their super powers." She emphasized Anna's term for the rats, gesturing air quotes with her fingers.

"No problem with my experiments," Hong Jin said, brushing aside his dark hair, which fell over his eyes.

"What about the first project I gave you, Anna? How's that going?"

Don's question brought her back to the present. At moments like this she felt as if she were being judged... and coming up short. Her heart sank; she had been neglecting this project, devoting her time instead to her super sniffers. At the rate she was going, it would take a year before she had enough data for a publication. Don jutted his neck forward towards her, forcing her to look at him. She stuttered a reply, reassuring him that she was making progress, albeit slowly.

He sat back in his chair and lapsed into his Mafia voice. "Well, you know how it goes. No data, no conference. Sorry, but that's how this *cosa nostra* works."

The meeting broke up, and Anna returned to her office. She slumped into her chair and stared mindlessly out the window. The weather had become hot and humid in the previous two weeks so she decided to postpone cycling back to her apartment until later in the evening when it had cooled down a little. While she didn't have a particularly high opinion of Tracy, there might be something to the idea that noise could disrupt a rat's estrus cycle. Three hours of online searching later she had learned that, whereas noise had no impact on their cycle, photoperiod did. According to several reports, the biggest external disruptor of a rat's estrus cycle was turning the lights on and off in their room each day.

Before leaving, she decided to check on the rats. The corridor was deserted when she swiped her ID card through the reader at the entrance to the animal housing facility. Inside, the steady hum of machinery maintaining the temperature and humidity in the suite of rooms was the only sound. With another swipe of her card, she opened the door to the room that housed the female rats. She had brought a flashlight, as the room was programmed for lights-out at 6 p.m.; they would come on again in the morning at 6. To her surprise, the room was brightly lit. Her watch showed 8:43 p.m. The timer was located at eye-level on the wall beside the door, a mechanical device in a box with a metal cover. Opening the box, she shone her flashlight beam on the trippers. One was set for lights-off at midnight, the other for lights-on at 6. Clearly, something had gone wrong. She quickly re-set the timer to its original schedule, and for a few minutes she stood in the dark listening to the rustle of activity from the cages. Then she tiptoed to the door, closed it gently behind her, and headed for home.

The animal-care staff were surprised to see Anna already there the following morning when they came to work. She had spent an almost sleepless night considering her options and rehearsing the language she would use. She didn't want to accuse anyone but rather establish who set the timers in each room and how often they were checked. Maybe it was just an oversight, or perhaps the timer in her room had failed. But these old mechanical timers were remarkably reliable. Within a few minutes it became clear to her that the animal-care staff never touched the timers. This was not in their job description; they considered this the responsibility of the researcher.

Back in her office Anna waited impatiently for Don to arrive. He barely had time to remove his jacket before she knocked on his office door.

"What's it now?" he snapped, turning his back to her and sitting down at his computer.

She told him about her literature search and what she had discovered—that a change in day length could disrupt the rats' cycle.

"I checked the room last night. The timer was set for lights-off at midnight. No wonder my experiments stopped working. I don't know how it could have happened, but I've re-set the timer to the old schedule, 6 a.m. and 6 p.m. Hopefully, the rats will get back to their regular cycle quickly and I get on with my experiments."

"Good." He gave her a dismissive nod.

Returning to the office she shared with Tracy and Hong Jin, Anna told them about the previous evening and explained that she had re-set the timer. Hong Jin thanked her politely.

"Well, *my* experiments are okay," Tracy said with a shrug of her shoulders. "You're the only one who seems to be having problems."

Anna was relieved when four out of six female rats showed their super powers the next time she ran the experiment. Returning them to the animal-care facility, she considered the two outliers; perhaps they needed another few days to synchronize their cycles with the rest of the animals in the room. Turning from the racks of cages, she opened the door on the timer mechanism and was stunned to see the mechanical trip set for lights-off at 11 p.m. The lights-on trip was set at 3 a.m. The rats would get four hours of darkness instead of their usual twelve. She could feel her heart thumping in her chest. There was no other explanation: someone was trying to sabotage her experiments.

She couldn't face returning to the lab. Stepping outside the building, a wave of sweltering heat assaulted her, forcing her to seek shelter in the Health Sciences library where she bought a coffee. Sitting with her back to the lobby, she hunched over the mug, trying to sort through her options. There was no reason to suspect the animal care staff. They already told her they didn't touch the timers. It must be somebody in her lab, but who? Don was out of the question. If he wanted to get rid of her, he could dismiss her at any time; postdocs had no job security. The undergraduates and graduate students seemed unlikely. The former didn't know enough, and graduate students were not going to do anything that might jeopardize their PhD. No, Anna reasoned, it must be one of the postdocs. But which one, Hong Jin or Tracy? She took another sip of coffee, which was rapidly cooling and becoming bitter.

Hong Jin was ambitious. He had an undergraduate degree in neuroscience from one of the most prestigious universities in China—Peking University—and like many of his compatriots had chosen to do postdoctoral training in the United States. She had the impression he wanted to return to China when he finished his postdoc and set up his own research lab there. Many Chinese scientists had similar ambitions, so he would have to be especially productive to succeed. All the same, she couldn't see how sabotaging her research would help him achieve his goals.

Something in her gut told her it was Tracy. Tracy, who sucked up to Don. Tracy, who wasn't that bright, just good at doing what she was told. Perhaps that was why Don had hired her, Anna thought. Someone who would greet you with a smile every morning and offer to get your coffee for you. Someone who remembered your birthday, even baked a cake for the occasion. Someone who agreed with everything you said and treated you like the Mafia Don you believed you were.

It was disheartening. Women weren't meant to betray other women, above all in science where their chance of success was already handicapped. Comparing herself with Tracy as dispassionately as she could, Anna began to understand a possible motive. Tracy didn't see Hong Jin as a competitor; after all, he was a foreigner and would eventually leave the country. Anna was different— an American just like her, but more intelligent. Anna's failure would allow Tracy to re-establish her position in the pecking order of the lab as the favorite. The problem was how to convince Don. He'd never believe Anna if she accused Tracy of sabotaging her experiments. She would have to present him with irrefutable proof.

Back in her office, Anna threw her lab coat on her chair and walked towards the door. Tracy and Hong Jin were both at their desks, their white-coated backs to her like cardboard cut-outs of what a scientist should look like. Tracy turned around.

"How did your experiment go today?" Tracy asked, her innocent expression framed by her dark hair with its pixie haircut.

Anna hesitated before answering. If she told the truth, would Tracy consider that a success or a failure?

"Not bad," she said with a smile. "Five out of six did really well. I think things are getting back on track."

On an impulse she added, "I've asked the guys in animal care to keep an eye on the timer in case it goes on the fritz again. They said they'd check it when they leave each afternoon."

Two days later Amazon Prime delivered a box to Anna's apartment. In the interim she had worked out exactly where to place the tiny camera. Attached to the vertical support of a cage rack and hidden behind a bag of rat chow, the camera lens would point towards the timer beside the door of the rat room. She wasn't sure whether everyone who came into the room would be imaged, but anyone who tampered with the timer surely would activate the motion detection system. The camera also had a date and time stamp, so she need not worry about the animal care staff checking the timer as they left each day. Anna's plan was to check the timer each morning to see if it had been tampered with, and if so, download the images on the memory card.

§

It took her almost a month to be certain. Only then did Anna raise the issue with Don, and as she expected, he didn't believe her. She forced him to look at the spreadsheet open on her laptop and pointed to a column of figures, before switching to a series of black and white images.

"Look at the data, Don. I have time-stamped images of Tracy doing something to the timer on these days. She came into the room between 5:00 and 7:00 each time. The staff go home at 4:30, and they know to check the timer before they leave."

Don pressed the left and right arrow keys reluctantly, going back and forth between the images.

"It *could* be Tracy...but all I'm seeing is the back of someone in a white coat with short dark hair."

Anna's voice rose in frustration.

"Don, it's a person doing something to the timer. My experiments have been all over the place for the past month. So, tell me, what else are they doing if not altering the timer. I've been going in every morning for the past three weeks, before the animal care staff turn up. It's there on the spreadsheet. Every time that person shows up, the lighting schedule is altered. What more do you need?" She shouted the last few words.

For several minutes he didn't say anything, instead toggling between images and the spreadsheet. Then he banged his fist down on the desk.

"Shit! This is the last thing I need to deal with. What did I say about never working with females. Rats, humans. I don't care."

Anna gave him her most withering look but realized that it was wasted. A part of her wanted to walk away from it all and find a different career, something that enabled women as opposed to denigrating them, a place of collaboration, not cutthroat competition. Was there such a place, she wondered? The irony of her situation was that she had deliberately chosen a career in academia because of its reputation as a gender-neutral meritocracy.

"So, what are you going to do about it?" she asked.

She wasn't going to let him backpedal or brush it aside.

"Will you call in the campus police?" she persisted.

"Whaaat? No, of course not! I'll have a talk with her." He looked past Anna, in the direction of the office the postdocs shared.

"But surely what she's done is illegal?" Anna persisted.

He cleared his throat.

"I'm not certain there's enough evidence to call in the police," he said, shaking his head.

Anna had been expecting him to prevaricate. She had one more idea but would need his cooperation.

"You've probably forgotten, but there's a log somewhere of every time someone goes into that room. We swipe our ID cards; the door won't open otherwise. Those records must be stored somewhere on campus and available...to you at least. For God's sake, PETA probably has access to them! If you compare the records with my spreadsheet and images, I'm sure you'll have enough to go to the police, or the Dean, or whoever you have to bring this to. I'm not letting this go, Don. This is my career at stake."

She glared at him, refusing to blink or drop her

gaze. She knew he wanted her to back down, but she was adamant. He let out a long sigh.

"Okay. Okay. I'll find out what's in the entry log for the room. Send me your spreadsheet. It'll take some time...I've got to go through channels, you understand. I'll get back to you."

"I'll not giving up, Don. I'll be checking the timer every morning until I know it's over and my project is safe."

She closed her laptop and turned to leave. At the door to his office she paused, waiting for him to look up.

"And if you don't go to the Dean, I will," she said, her voice cold and dispassionate.

Anna avoided her office as much as possible for the next several days. Instead, she concentrated on her bread-and-butter project, spending much of the time in the microscope room or working in the library. To her relief Don canceled the weekly lab meeting with the excuse that he had a scheduling conflict. It wasn't until ten days later when Anna, dropping her purse off in her office before going to the microscope room, noticed that Tracy's desk had been cleared.

She marched into Don's office and without preamble asked, "What happened?"

"You were right," her said. "Her ID card was swiped every single time the timer was altered. She denied it, of course. Said that she had lost her card a few months ago and got a replacement."

He sighed. "God, I hate this stuff. It's been a nightmare. You've no idea what I've had to go through."

Without Tracy around, Anna thought cynically, Don

no longer has his reliable sycophant. But she refused to step into Tracy's shoes.

"How do you think I feel?" she said. "After all, I'm the one who lost months of data, and now I'm going to have to repeat all of those experiments."

They glared at each other across the desk.

"So, what happened? Is she going to jail?" Anna demanded.

"The university has decided not to press charges. It wouldn't look good on the front page of the Gainesville Press...and PETA would have a field day with it. Her animal use privileges have been suspended indefinitely. What that means is she cannot do any experiments, at least not with animals. So she's no use to me."

He sat back in his chair and folded his arms. "She's decided to leave the lab...of her own volition."

This pronouncement was followed by an awkward silence, during which Anna considered whether to pursue the topic but decided against it. She really didn't care what became of Tracy.

"Well, I'd better get back to my rats," she said, turning to leave the room.

"Um..." Don's voice trailed off, but it was clear to Anna that he had something more to say. She came back and stood in front of his desk, waiting.

"Well, the thing is...we've lost a lot of time. I cannot afford to have you spend another six months on your super sniffers, or whatever you call them. The females. I want you to take over Tracy's project."

Anna stared at him, her mouth falling open. She

felt numb. He held his hands up, palms open, and gave an exaggerated shrug. This was Don in Mafia boss mode.

"Hey, science is a business. I have to show progress or my grant won't get renewed. Right now, I need some publications. Tracy's project is almost there. It just needs a few more experiments and it'll be ready for writing up. You'd be first author. Tracy will have to be on the manuscript of course...."

He looked up to see her reaction before continuing.

"You'll be the senior author. A publication in the first year of your postdoc—that's going to look good on your CV." He paused for effect before adding, "Otherwise, I'll have to give the project to Hong Jin."

She could feel her heart thumping in her chest.

She heard herself say, "Okay."

"That's settled then," he said with finality. "I'm glad it's all over." He turned to face his computer, dismissing her.

She walked slowly back to her office, stunned by Don's bluntness. Hong Jin looked up as she came into the room. It was impossible to read his expression, and in any case, he wasn't someone whose shoulder she could cry on. She was an adult, she reminded herself, not a child whose trip to Disney World had just been canceled. But the super sniffers *had* been her Disney World, her own Marvel characters, and now they were gone. She logged on to the Society for Neuroscience web page and went through the instructions for recalling her abstract. With a final key stroke, her territorial claim was obliterated. Between now and when I eventually set up my own lab, would anyone else discover that female rats had super powers, she wondered? Would anyone steal her idea?

Hong Jin was still looking at her.

"I'm sorry," he said.

Anna nodded and got up from her desk to leave. At the door she looked back, noticing for the first time how Hong Jin's short, dark hair tapered to a point just above the collar of his white coat. The truth slammed into her, filling her with shock and disgust. As she rushed to the building entrance, her mind went back over every single detail of the past few weeks. It all fit: the timing, the images she had captured, Tracy's lost ID, and above all, a motive. He had recognized that her super sniffers were a real breakthrough—a project he wanted to pursue when he opened his own lab. She had been wrong about Tracy and now the girl's career was ruined. At best Tracy might get a job as a technician in a laboratory; more likely she would leave science forever. Anna had killed her future.

A flurry of ideas went through Anna's mind. Perhaps there was still time to do something about it? She could tell Don she had made a mistake, but he wouldn't want to listen. For him the matter was closed. Besides, she had no proof that Hong Jin was the saboteur. He had been careful and patient—hallmarks of a good scientist. With a sinking feeling, Anna realized that she was not going to do or say anything. In the future, Hong Jin would become a respected colleague, a reviewer of her manuscripts and grant applications. They might even collaborate.

As she walked towards the bike rack, Anna's thoughts were already shifting to Tracy's near-complete project and the coveted slot of first author.

A Safe Place

The summer storm arrived with little warning, sweeping across Lake Kegonsa with surprising ferocity. A flash of lightning illuminated the skyline followed immediately by a crash of thunder that reverberated around the apartment like an explosion. The room was plunged into darkness, and the smoke detector chirruped plaintively as if newly awoken.

Sitting on the screened-in porch, Chris peered across the lake where lights from the hospital on the opposite shore glowed eerily. He groped his way back inside the apartment, to the kitchen where he remembered there was a candle and a box of matches in one of the drawers. Returning to the porch, he lit the candle and set it down on an ashtray, anchoring it with a dollop of hot wax. There was nothing to do but sit in the semi-darkness and wait. He had made his decision weeks ago, but there never seemed to be an opportune time to tell Mark, his partner for the past three years. He slumped into the wicker loveseat and began to rehearse what he was going to say when Mark returned from his weekly poker session, most likely drunk. Each time Chris tried out the speech there seemed to be fewer and fewer words until he was left with just two: it's over.

Staring at the tiny point of light, Chris inhaled the odor of beeswax. Once upon a time the unctuous fragrance would have conjured an image of his boyhood church in Great Falls, Montana, with its comforting rituals. Instead, he found himself thinking of the place where he had been the happiest in his life.

§

The letter from the World Wildlife Fund arrived at the start of his fourth year in graduate school at Cornell, informing Chris that his grant application to study the behavior of giant anteaters in the Amazon basin had been approved. Numbers of giant anteaters had declined precipitously over the past decade due to habitat destruction, and the species was now listed as vulnerable. He was to fly to Guyana in October and spend ten weeks in the south of the country in a region considered to be one of the last great wildernesses on the planet, the Rupununi. His girlfriend at the time was not at all pleased. She hadn't wanted him to apply for the grant; he would miss her sister's wedding when she planned to introduce him to her family. But he persuaded her that this was a once-in-a-lifetime opportunity, and it would look good on his resume when it came to applying for faculty positions. Susan and he had been dating for a little over a year and planned to move in together the following January. Susan had found an apartment within walking distance of the campus library where she worked, and although Chris loved the ramshackle farmhouse he was renting on the outskirts of Ithaca, her logic was unassailable. They would be able to pay off their student loans early and begin to save for a house. Susan had abundant plans for their future, and while Chris went along with most of them, sometimes he wondered if he was truly in love with Susan.

Three weeks later Chris was on a flight from New York's JFK airport to Guyana. The other white men on the flight were seated in Business Class whereas he found himself in the main cabin surrounded by cheerful and talkative Afro-Guyanese women going home on vacation. Eavesdropping on the three women in the row behind, he listened to a discussion of the merits of Flash as a floor cleaner and how to cook a particular Guyanese dish if you were unable to find the ingredients in Queens. Nurses, nannies, teachers, and cleaners, these women exuded happiness, and he felt a pang of loneliness as he watched them disperse into the welcoming arms of their families at Georgetown airport.

His first impressions of the country were discouraging. The capital city had an air of neglect, with run-down buildings and streets littered with plastic bags, soda bottles, and beer cans. The heat was overwhelming, as if a hot wet blanket had been dropped on the city, trapping the nauseating stench from smoldering piles of garbage that dotted the sidewalks. I can survive this heat for ten weeks, Chris thought, already looking forward to winter back in Ithaca.

His spirits lifted a little when his taxi pulled up in front of the Pegasus Hotel, a Georgetown landmark overlooking the coastline. He felt a momentary pang of guilt as he stepped into the air-conditioned lobby but shrugged it off, reasoning that life would be very different where he was going. Tomorrow he would fly to Lethem, a small town in the south of the country on the Brazilian border, and from there travel overland to an isolated cattle ranch in the middle of the Rupununi, a place called Dadanawa.

That evening he decided to splurge on a meal at the hotel, and as most of the poolside tables were occupied, took a seat at the bar. Struggling to be heard over the din of pulsating music, Chris shouted his order to the barman, with an apologetic look to a man sitting farther along the bar. The man responded with a rueful smile, raised his glass by way of acknowledgement, and mouthed something that was immediately lost in the cacophony. Chris shook his head from side to side and cupped his hand to his ear, whereupon the man picked up his glass and moved to the bar stool next to Chris. Their knees touched briefly.

Gesturing to the band playing by the pool, the man said, "*Limin* is what they call it—partying Caribbean style. Lots of liquor and music and dancing."

Chris turned in his seat and watched as two of the hotel staff began to clear the area directly in front of the musicians that would serve as the dance floor. His new companion touched Chris's bare arm, the fingers lingering a fraction longer than necessary.

"See, I told you. The dancing will be starting soon," he said, giving Chris a knowing look.

The man was slightly shorter than Chris, around six feet, with the muscular definition of someone who works out regularly. Chris guessed that he was about thirty-five, although his smile made him look younger. He was wearing a pale green shirt, open at the neck and tucked into tailored black trousers. Hanging from a leather thong around his neck was a jade pendant, the pale green contrasting with his dark chest. Chris couldn't help wondering what blend of genes was buried in the man's ancestry. They introduced themselves, their heads almost touching as they struggled to be heard over the music. To Chris's surprise Roy was South African, working in Guyana as a mining consultant. His contract allowed him to spend one week each month in Georgetown at the company's headquarters—a welcome respite from the rough-and-ready gold mining camps in the interior of the country, he assured Chris. Chris raised his hand to order another beer, but the gesture was interrupted by Roy who grabbed his wrist and pushed it back down onto the bar.

"You have to try El Dorado," Roy insisted. "It's the local rum. Trust me—it's like nothing you've ever had before."

His breath tickled pleasantly as he spoke the words into Chris's ear. Chris grinned and nodded, whereupon Roy ordered two shots of twelve-year old El Dorado. Based on the barman's careful pour, this was not a drink to be tossed back lightly, and Chris sipped appreciatively, rolling the smoky liquid around his mouth before swallowing.

"Let's go somewhere where we can hear ourselves," Roy said, his voice barely audible over the band that had turned up the volume on their amplifiers now that the dancing had started. "The Palm Court should still be fairly quiet, although it gets noisier as the night goes on. It's only a few blocks from here." Taking Chris's elbow, he guided him past the dance floor and out onto the street. A taxi slowed, but Roy waved it on.

That night in Georgetown with Roy was not Chris's first homosexual encounter. Since adolescence he'd had an inkling that his compass needle did not always orient towards north. Nonetheless, his Catholic high school in Great Falls was not a place to encourage exploration of sexual identity, and he graduated unsure whether he was straight, gay, or bisexual. College offered more opportunities to inquire, but he was fundamentally shy, preferring bird-watching and fishing to dating. In the end he settled for a girl called Susan, someone whom he could bring home to his conservative parents and make them happy. Neither Susan nor any of his friends knew that he cruised gay bars when he had the opportunity, usually while attending scientific meetings in distant cities. Terrifying and exhilarating, these encounters had become a necessary part of his life.

He left Roy's room at dawn and took a quick shower before going to the airport. He wasn't looking forward to the flight in a small propeller airplane, but managed to fall asleep shortly after takeoff. The bumpy landing brought him back to reality, and he looked out the window searching for a sign that they had reached their destination. Beyond the grass strip there was nothing—just more grassland that stretched into the distance. Two middle-aged American women got off the plane looking relieved when a jeep drove up to meet them. As the plane rose back into the sky, Chris wondered where the women were going; he could see no sign of a village or even a hut, just endless savanna. Only once did he see what looked like a road, a line of orange-brown dirt snaking its way through the grassland. Up to now he had gone along with the detailed instructions provided by the World Wildlife Fund about getting to Dadanawa, giving little thought as to what lay ahead. Now, looking down at the vast empty landscape, he experienced a moment of panic. There were no instructions as to what he should do once he arrived at his destination.

They landed on a paved runway at Lethem, over an hour late. A dust-covered Land Cruiser—its air intake capped by a snorkel—was parked just outside the wire fence surrounding the airport, the door open as if waiting for someone. Chris walked towards the vehicle, hesitated, then lowered his backpack to the ground. A dark-skinned Amerindian man emerged from a nearby building, a bottle of Stag beer in his hand.

"You Chris Franklin?" he asked.

Chris nodded, trying not to show his relief.

"You need anything before we leave town? It's four hours to Dadanawa."

"A bottle of water, perhaps," Chris replied, and the man jerked his thumb back towards the building.

"In there. They've got a toilet too."

Boxes of groceries filled the back of the Land Cruiser, and Chris ended up squeezing his backpack into the space by his feet. On the way out of town they pulled into a gas station where, in addition to fueling the Land Cruiser, the driver filled three large jerrycans, which he hoisted effortlessly onto the roof rack and strapped down next to a rusty gas cylinder.

"I'd tie your pack up there but it's going to rain," he said. "Better to keep it inside."

Back on the deserted road, a line of red dirt from which narrow tracks led off every few miles, the driver introduced himself as Manni. Conversation was difficult over the roar of the engine, especially as Manni spoke softly, barely enunciating the words. They passed a solitary motorcycle going in the opposite direction laden with packages, and a little while later, three Amerindian women who looked as if they were out for an afternoon stroll, despite there being no sign of a village. Just as Chris was beginning to drift off into an uncomfortable sleep, they pulled up beside a small, brick building surrounded by a few palm-covered huts. The roar of the Land Cruiser engine was replaced by the throbbing sound of a generator.

"You want a beer?" Manni asked.

Thus far the journey had been uncomfortably hot and dusty, and the prospect of a warm beer was not at all appealing. Nonetheless, Chris nodded and followed Manni into the shanty where several people were drinking and conversing in a language Chris didn't recognize but which Manni explained was Macushi. He seemed to know everyone. To Chris's surprise the beer was ice cold, and he held the bottle to his face, rolling it over his hot cheeks before taking a welcome gulp. Everyone laughed.

Soon after they resumed their journey, the sky clouded over and within minutes there was a torrential downpour that washed the accumulated dust from the windshield. By now the road had shrunk to little more than a track, and the Land Cruiser plunged through puddles of water that splattered against the sides of the vehicle. A few minutes later they stopped abruptly. The narrow track ended at a muddy bank, and in front of them was a wide, fast-flowing river. It seemed impossible to cross, and there was no sign of a ferry. Manni waded into the water up to his thighs, paused for a minute or more, then returned to the Land Cruiser. There was a grating sound as he engaged the four-wheel drive, took one more look to his left and right, and to Chris's amazement drove straight into the river. A knot of panic rose in Chris's chest as he watched the water swirl around the doors, almost reaching the window. He felt confident he could squeeze through the open window if they capsized but wasn't sure he would be able to swim to shore before being swept away. And weren't there piranha in these rivers? He held his breath as Manni steered the vehicle downstream, angled left towards a sandbar dotted with scrubby trees, then turned upstream, the tires alternately gripping and sliding on submerged rocks. When the Land Cruiser eventually found traction in the muddy bank on the opposite shore, Chris let out an audible sigh.

"That was amazing."

"The river's low. There'll be fishing tomorrow," Manni said, flashing him a smile.

The last few hundred yards were across open ground where a scattering of cattle grazed, indifferent to their arrival. They approached a cluster of buildings, behind which towered a water pump windmill, and stopped at a two-story building surrounded by a high veranda. A figure leaned over the railing, her freckled face framed by a corona of unruly red hair. She looks to be about fourteen, Chris thought, and wondered who she was. A few moments later she stood before him, her hand thrust out.

"Welcome to Dadanawa, Chris. I'm Bridget"

She was wearing an old-fashioned summer dress that came below her knees, and he noticed she was barefoot. Grabbing his pack by the straps, she slung it over her shoulder and began to climb back up the stairs. He followed, protesting.

"This is your room," she said, opening a door off the veranda. "It's small, but you can hang out anywhere up here." She gestured towards the wide deck where several Adirondack chairs and tables were scattered around, together with hammocks. "There's a bathroom down the hall. Cold water only, but the water is safe. We pump it from a deep well. You'll hear the generator running for a couple of hours each day."

Bridget lowered his pack to the floor and stepped out onto the veranda.

"Would you like some tea and cake? Dinner won't be until sunset."

Although he was hot and sweaty and yearning for a shower, Bridget's Scottish accent piqued his curiosity and he agreed to join her. Laid out on a white tablecloth in one corner of the veranda were two cups and saucers, a thermos, and a fruit cake covered with a linen napkin. Chris couldn't help smiling at the incongruity—as if he had arrived at an English country house in time for afternoon tea. Bridget poured, and they settled into an easy conversation. He discovered that she was married to Leslie, the owners' son, who was nominally in charge of the ranch, together with his sister Jelissa, while their parents spent a few months in Canada. Just now there were no guests, but a German family was expected the following day.

"They'll be staying at the guest house," Bridget said, pointing to a building about fifty yards to the west. "You can go out with them in the jeep if you like. Or you could take one of the horses. Do you ride?"

"I do, actually," said Chris. "I used to spend summers on my grandfather's ranch in Montana, so I'm pretty comfortable around horses."

"That's good to hear. Otherwise you might have had to take a bicycle for your field trips." She laughed, her eyes dancing with mirth. "Auntie Joy will look after you.... She'll find you a good horse."

They finished their tea and Bridget carried the tray downstairs. When she didn't reappear after several minutes, Chris went to his room, pulled aside the mosquito netting hanging over the bed, and lay down. Within a few minutes he was fast asleep.

He woke at sunrise, his mind alert to the absence of man-made sounds. Instead, there were bird calls, and in the background he could hear cattle lowing plaintively. Pushing aside the mosquito net, he climbed out of bed, stepped out onto the veranda, and leaned on the railing. The fronds of two tall palm trees framed a perfect view: miles of savanna that ended in a range of low hills, their colors developing gradually in the morning light. Below the veranda, pigs and sheep foraged in the scrubby grass alongside a flock of ducks. Two dogs trotted by with a purposeful air, and in the distance, he could see a figure on horseback. Chris felt as if he had stepped into a movie, *Out of Africa* perhaps, or the Australian outback in the 1950s. He took a brief cold shower and went downstairs to the dining room where he found breakfast laid out, the plates of food covered carefully with cloth napkins.

Bridget found him later and offered to show him around the ranch. Today she was wearing a short, colorful summer dress and her hair had been braided into two thick plaits that rested easily on her breasts. Once again, she was barefoot, and he noticed a thin woven leather anklet on her left leg. She apologized that Leslie wasn't around, but he had gone to Georgetown to take delivery of a new John Deere tractor that had been shipped from India.

"Depending on the state of the road, it could take him a week to get back. Crossing the Demerara River could be a problem, and then there's the Essequibo, though Manni said it isn't bad right now."

"Why India?" Chris asked, as he mentally calculated the distance between the two countries. "Couldn't he get a tractor from...well, some place nearer?"

"Indian ones don't have so much computer stuff," she said, gesturing to the numerous rusting vehicles that were scattered around the yard. "We need to be able to repair everything ourselves."

Followed by her dog, a lean mongrel she introduced as Piglet, she made her way towards a cluster of buildings behind the main lodge, indifferent to the clods of dried dung that littered the scrubby grass. Dadanawa was not just a working ranch, and an ecotourist destination, but a village of some twenty or thirty people, most of them Amerindian, Bridget explained. Some families lived in their own houses, while others shared accommodations. She pointed out the bunk house where the vaqueros lived—cowboys who looked after the cattle and horses. The men usually spent two weeks at the ranch, then took a few days off, returning to their own villages scattered throughout the Rupununi.

"It's different in the rainy season...December and January. You'll miss it, I think. We're totally isolated here then. The road to Lethem washes out in places and the river is too high to get across. Kids still go to school though. People use canoes and dugouts to get around."

"What's that?" Chris asked, pointing to a cowhide stretched across a spindly frame, propped upright under a corrugated metal awning. For a moment he thought it might be some sort of art project.

"We slaughter a cow every few weeks, eat as much as we can, and salt and dry the rest. I hope you're not vegetarian. You can expect beef at every meal here."

She walked over to the cowhide and patted it affectionately. "Uncle Grenison tans the hides. He repairs all the horse tack too, although he's getting old so one of Auntie Joy's sons is learning how."

They continued walking, eventually coming to a long, low, brick building with a metal roof. Wooden benches and a couple of metal chairs lined the outside wall, and over the half door hung a sign, Dadanawa General Store. Inside, beneath shelves stocked with everything imaginable for a household, were sacks of rice and flour, and crates of the ubiquitous Stag beer.

Bridget pointed to a large chest freezer against one wall, below which a collection of large batteries stood on the floor, loosely connected by a tangle of electrical cables.

"It's solar powered, so it's not great. But it keeps the beer cold, and we usually get a little ice for drinks at night."

Chris asked whether he would be able to charge his computer.

"It might take longer than you're used to, but it'll work. There's no internet though. We have a short-wave radio for emergencies. If you're desperate, you can always go into Lethem when we pick up guests and use the public phone there."

Walking back to the lodge, Chris discovered that Bridget had originally come to Guyana from Edinburgh on her gap year to teach at a school on the road between Lethem and Dadanawa. She fell in love with the place and the people, but above all, with Leslie. Their relationship had survived the four years she spent at university in England studying Geology, he visiting her as often as he could manage. When she graduated, she took a job with a mining company in Guyana, allowing her to return to Dadanawa for a week each month. After a year, she moved to the ranch permanently. To Chris it seemed such a radical decision, and yet clearly, she was happy. There was an air of carefree delight about her, so different from Susan, who always appeared anxious. He envied Bridget and wished he could be more like her.

Over the weeks that followed, Chris too fell in love with the Rupununi and its people. There was a sense of patience and tolerance, as if the land didn't conform to the rules of time. Plans were constantly being disrupted, but instead of becoming frustrated, people would say, "You can't fight life," delivering the Macushi words with a shrug and a smile. He envied these people's lives, in balance with each other and the land.

Life was reduced to its essence, the pulse of each day dictated by the passage of the sun. If there were guests, he joined them on an early morning "safari" together with Leslie and one or two Amerindian guides, whose knowledge of the terrain, flora, and fauna never ceased to amaze him. He tried to learn as much as he could about giant anteaters from them, and spent hours writing down everything he could remember. As the morning heated up, there might be a canoe trip down the Rupununi River with its rich bird life, followed by a swim, before returning to the ranch for a cold beer. Lunch was the main meal of the day, after which everyone retired to their quarters and slept for a couple of hours. On days when there were no guests, in the afternoon Chris would take one of the horses for a long ride, secure in the knowledge that the animal would find its way back to the ranch by sundown. If he chanced upon an Amerindian house, he was sure of a warm greeting, a beer, and a place to sling his hammock.

There was always something to watch at the corrals:

horses being broken in, calves branded and tattooed, and cattle selected for the market in Lethem, a week-long round trip. But the highlight for Chris was watching the vaqueros practice for the annual Lethem rodeo. These men were short in stature but surprisingly strong, easily lassoing a cow or steer and roping it into submission, after which they would ride the animal bareback. It reminded him of Junior Rodeo in Montana, only these men strutted around the corral in the most magnificent chaps he had ever seen—tanned jaguar hides. Initially he was appalled by their flaunting of an endangered species. But Leslie explained to him that when jaguar preyed on cattle close to a ranch, they were considered too dangerous to tolerate and shot.

After a few weeks, Chris plucked up his courage and asked Manni if he could try his hand at roping.

"I used to do rodeo back home in Montana," he said, and not sure whether Manni had understood added, "I've done tie-down roping and steer wrestling...and a bit of bull riding." Listening to himself, he felt a little embarrassed. After all, here were real cattlemen, not some college kid who pretended to be a bronco-buster in his summer vacation.

Manni walked away, and Chris wished he hadn't said anything. But he soon returned with a pair of chaps and leather gloves, handing them to Chris with a grin. The chaps were old and worn but serviceable, and he buckled them on with a growing sense of excitement, conscious that everyone was looking at him. He missed on his first attempt, but managed on the second try to get a rope around a young steer's neck. Manni joined him in the corral, expertly roping the steer's fore and hind limbs.

Three more men joined them, bringing it to the ground and tying a rope around its flank. Chris stepped over the steer, grabbed the flank rope, nodded to the men that he was ready, and braced himself for the explosive thrust as the steer was freed of its tethers and righted itself. His triumph lasted five seconds before he was flung to the ground. The vaqueros shouted and clapped when he got up, dusted himself off, and walked to the corral fence to join Bridget and a few of the guests who had come to watch. His shoulder was on fire and his knees were bruised, but none of it mattered. He felt a kinship with everyone present; he was beginning to belong at Dadanawa.

There was a magical ritual to evenings at the ranch house. Like moths drawn to a flame, guests made their way to the veranda and settled themselves into chairs or hammocks while Bridget handed around glasses of rum diluted with fruit juice, each with a precious sliver of ice. Conversations usually began with what animals and plants the guests had spotted that day; many of the guests were well-travelled and knowledgeable, and Chris incorporated their data into his field notes. Having no other form of entertainment, conversation was an important part of the lifestyle, all subjects being legitimate topics. With only a single candle flame burning, the voices that emerged from the darkness had a degree of anonymity, which often enlivened the exchanges but also allowed for surprisingly intimate confessions. Occasionally, Chris joined in, but sometimes he would lie in a hammock far from the group, allowing the words to flow past him as he stared into the star-filled sky.

One evening when everyone had left the veranda

except Bridget, Chris found himself talking to her about Susan. By now he and Bridget had become friends, thrown together by Leslie's frequent absences, and Chris's need for answers to endless questions about the Rupununi. Earlier that afternoon Chris had written a letter to Susan, the first since leaving Ithaca four weeks earlier. Leslie would be driving to Lethem the following day to pick up some guests and had offered to mail it for him. Chris had struggled to write more than couple of pages. It wasn't that he hadn't anything to tell her; his days were filled with people and stories and endless new experiences. He just didn't want to share any of his life at Dadanawa with her. He had hesitated before signing the letter, 'Love, Chris', knowing that if he omitted the sentiment, she would be hurt. Even so, the prospect of seeing her when he returned to the United States filled him with apprehension. He realized that he didn't want to share a future with her but had no idea how to extricate himself. His anguished confession spilled out into the darkness as he wiped the tears from his eyes.

"What would you do if you were me?" he asked.

Bridget sighed. "I suppose I wouldn't have let it get this far."

She moved to sit beside him on the wicker loveseat and took his hands in hers.

"You'll have to tell her sooner or later. It's not fair to lead her along like this." Her voice was gentle in the darkness. "It'll break her heart, but she'll get over it."

Chris yearned for Bridget to cradle his head against her breast, stroke his cheek, and envelop him in her arms.

She was everything he wanted in a woman—if that's what he truly wanted.

"Don't worry. You'll work it out," she said, replacing his hands in his own lap and getting up to leave.

§

Chris heard the door to the apartment open followed by a light switch being flicked on and off several times.

"Shit!"

Mark's voice traveled up the stairs, followed by the sound of his footsteps. He lurched onto the porch and slumped down on the loveseat beside Chris, who shifted slightly, recoiling from the smell of stale beer and cigarettes. They sat for several minutes, neither willing to launch the conversation that had been simmering for months.

It was Mark who spoke first.

"This isn't working, is it?" His words were slurred.

Chris let out a long sigh. "No. It's not."

"I suppose you want me to move out?"

"No. You stay. I'll go."

There was another long silence as Mark's muddled brain tried to absorb the implications of Chris's statement.

"Where'll you go?"

"I'm going back to Guyana."

Mark turned to look at Chris, his eyes trying to focus on the face of his lover. In the flickering light from the candle, he saw that Chris was looking out into the darkness, a serene expression on his face.

"To the place where you rode bulls?"

"Yeah. That place. Dadanawa."

"What'll you do there?"

"I'm not sure. Write up some papers. Collect more data. I'm on sabbatical next semester so it doesn't matter where I go."

There was another long pause.

"They've got internet at the ranch now," Chris said, not certain whether Mark was still listening or had fallen asleep.

"I didn't know you'd stayed in touch," Mark said.

"Yeah. We exchange emails every so often. Bridget and Leslie are still doing the ecotourist thing. I send them articles when I come across stuff about the Rupununi. They've got a kid now. There's a picture of him on their website, sitting on the corral fence. He was probably watching the vaqueros practice for rodeo. He's got red hair, and there's a big grin on his face."

Chris was smiling now, a wave of relief flooding into his heart. He was going home.

The School Reunion

The tinny sound of the letterbox flap, followed by a soft thud of envelopes falling on the hall floor must have caught James's attention because he appeared within seconds, brandishing his wand.

"Maxie, Maxie, Maxie," he shouted excitedly.

James was my grandson. I looked after him three days a week. My daughter lived a couple of miles away, so it was easy for her to drop him off at my house on her way to work. For the first few years her partner was able to look after James during the daytime—he worked the night shift. But recently his hours changed, and Laura asked if I could help out.

"It's just for a few months, and he'll be a bit of company for you. It must be lonely for you with Daddy gone."

Of course, I was lonely after Jack died, but a four-year-old wasn't going to change that. All the same, I agreed. Some days I looked forward to him coming over; other days I could kill the little monster. It was a mistake to buy the wand, but I thought it might focus James's attention when I read to him. He wasn't much interested in books, even ones the librarian suggested, so I decided to read the first Harry Potter to him. At least I would enjoy listening to the story again, I reasoned, and if he actually got into it, there are plenty more where that came from.

Maxie was our postman. When the letterbox opened each morning as if by magic, I used to say to James, "There's Maxie." Somehow the little fellow got it into his head that this was a spell, and now his version of *wingardium leviosa* was "Maxie, Maxie, Maxie," accompanied by a lot of wand waving in the direction of the front door.

We gathered the envelopes from the floor and took them into the kitchen. I always gave James the rejects to open; it kept him distracted while I sorted through the rest of the mail. That day he ripped the plastic cover off a holiday catalog and started to flip through the shiny pages, pausing occasionally to point at a colorful image, all the while babbling away to himself. Meanwhile, I picked up the envelope with the blue and red striped border. The handwriting was unfamiliar and the sender's name, Nuala Barnes, with an address in Perth, Australia, didn't mean anything to me. I slit the envelope open with a paring knife, but before I had a chance to satisfy my curiosity, James thrust the brochure up at me and demanded that I tell him a story. Much later, after Laura took him home that evening, I sat down at the kitchen table with a cup of tea, opened the letter, and began to read. It was quite a surprise.

Nuala Williams had been in my class at boarding school when we first went to the Sacred Heart Convent in Athlone at eleven years of age. The last time I saw her was over fifty years ago, the day we finished our final exams and were about to leave the place forever. Only Nuala wasn't. She was going right back into that convent and would be staying there for the rest of her life. A few years later I heard that she had been sent to Africa to teach at a school run by the nuns. After that, according to the letter I was holding in my hand, she was sent to Australia to teach at a girls' school in Perth.

Her handwriting was extraordinary, the cursive loops exaggerated as if she had deliberately chosen to deviate from the norm. The nuns had been rigid in their interpretation of how to write properly, and woe betide any of us who strove for originality. Nuala had broken ranks, it seemed, and not just with her cursive. She wrote that after a year in Perth, she had left the convent and married the father of one of her pupils, Ron Barnes. They had four children together, and she gave me an abbreviated version of their lives. How she found me after all this time was nothing short of a miracle. Somehow, the fact that my father was a butcher in Cork had stuck in her mind, so she wrote to a cousin of hers there, a veterinarian, and asked him to see if he could locate anyone in my family. Within a week she had my married name and my address in Dublin.

Towards the end of her letter, Nuala got to the point. Ron had just offered her a trip back to Ireland for her 70th birthday, and because she hadn't been home in nearly fifty years, he suggested she might want a little time by herself to catch up with relatives and friends. He would meet her afterwards in England where he had family, and they would continue on to France and Italy for the remainder of their vacation. Her next paragraph left me speechless.

"I'd love to get together with some of the girls who used to be in our class at school. You were the Head Girl, so I thought you might have stayed in contact with some of them. Is there any chance you could organize a get-together next summer?"

Our class was never one for reunions. The last time we got together was when the school closed its doors around thirty years ago. I kept in touch with a few of the girls but I didn't see them that often, so my initial reaction to Nuala's suggestion was not at all enthusiastic. Still, the more I thought about it the more the idea grew on me. We lost two of our class in the last year, both to cancer. That left twenty-eight of us hovering around the seventy mark with the clock ticking audibly.

Over the next few months, Nuala and I went back and forth by e-mail, picking a date and agreeing on a suitable venue. While I'd have preferred to meet in Dublin, many of the girls lived in the western half of the country, so it was going to have to be somewhere in the middle; Athlone was the obvious place. The town was not especially popular with tourists, but it was on the main railway line between Dublin and Galway and had a big conference hotel, the Radisson Blu. The irony of holding a reunion in Athlone didn't escape either of us. After all, we had spent six years of our lives cloistered in that small, provincial town, whose only claim to fame at the time was an enormous catholic church, Saints Peter and Paul, overlooking the Shannon River. At least I wouldn't have to organize a tour of our old school as the building had been demolished to make way for a shopping mall and condominiums.

§

I picked Nuala up from her hotel in Dublin at noon on Friday. I was afraid I wouldn't recognize her after all those years, but I needn't have worried. She looked just the same, tall and athletic, only with grey hair instead of the long brown braid that used to bounce behind her when she ran down the center of the hockey pitch. She'd been Captain of Sports in our last year at Sacred Heart, the year we won the Leinster school's hockey cup.

"You're wonderful!" she said, ignoring my out-stretched hand and giving me a hug. "I cannot thank you enough for organizing this."

She pulled back to get a better look at me, then hugged me to her again. I noticed her accent was different—she had lost the guttural Cork vowels, but the sweet shy smile I remembered was still there. Wearing a colorful, short-sleeved top and capri trousers, her skin had a weather-beaten look, and I wondered if that was from her time in Africa. The pictures of Sacred Heart nuns in Africa showed them wearing a full-length habit, albeit white instead of black, so I decided that she must live an outdoorsy kind of life in Australia. It was a good place to start the conversation, and as it turned out, she played a lot of golf. I was a keen golfer too, and that topic kept things rolling as we negotiated Dublin traffic. By the time we got to the beginning of the Galway motorway, we were at ease with one another, reminiscing about our time at Sacred Heart, each of us jogging the other's memory and filling in details that we had long ago forgotten. We chatted about who was coming to the reunion and with each girl's name, I gave her as much information as I knew about their subsequent lives.

"Is Josie Sheehan coming?" she asked.

"As far as I know she is. You were great friends with her at school, weren't you?"

"Yes, we were. But we lost touch. It will be good to see her again."

Our rooms at the Radisson weren't ready, so we took a stroll by the river where several trendy restaurants and bars had sprung up to take advantage of a renewed interest in the historic part of the town. I wanted more time with Nuala before I had to share her with the rest of our class, so when we came to Sean's Bar, which claimed to be Ireland's oldest pub, I suggested we go inside for a coffee. She gave a hearty laugh.

"A coffee? I'm ready for something stronger than that. It's going to be a long evening."

Nuala was sixteen when she told us she was going to be a nun. I remember the day clearly. We were in the refectory talking about what we were going to do after the Leaving Certificate exam. Someone said, "Let's go around the table," and girls chimed in with university, nursing, airhostess, teaching, and a few admitting they weren't sure yet. When it came to Nuala's turn, she told us that she had a vocation. Maybe it's because we were always surrounded by nuns, but none of us questioned her career choice.

I had been wanting to ask her a specific question since we left Dublin, but I was afraid I'd come across as rude. Now, as we raised our glasses of wine in unison, I finally said, "Why did you leave the convent?"

Her answer surprised me with its simplicity.

"I lost my faith."

The expression itself was familiar; the nuns at Sacred Heart would sometimes ask us to pray for people who had lost their faith. But back then I had no concept of what it meant. Nuala went on to describe how it felt— when she finally acknowledged that she no longer believed in God.

"The sense of loss is overwhelming. You feel utterly bereft, hollowed out, empty. It's an existential grief—a hell of sorts."

The expression on her face changed, as if she were reviewing the sequence of her life. First, there was pain, then sadness, then acceptance followed by hope and finally...it was hard to describe, but she looked beautiful. All the lines seem to leave her face except for the creases at the corners of her eyes. She took a sip of wine and continued with her story.

"I never thought about my faith when I was working in Africa. It all seemed so clear there. God had given me a task—to bring hope and love, and some English grammar and spelling too." She gave a little laugh.

"Australia was different. They didn't need hope or love in the Sacred Heart convent in Perth, just English and math. The senselessness of it all hit me one day and...I couldn't find my way back. I tried talking to Mother Superior about it but she had nothing to give me, no words of comfort or reassurance. She forbade me to talk about it to anyone in the convent. Looking back on it now, I suppose she was terrified that I might infect the other nuns with my 'disease.' My confessor was equally unhelpful. He had a bit of a misogynistic streak in him and was definitely not interested in discussing theology with a woman. Instead, he ordered me to go on a month-long silent retreat. I still taught classes, but the rest of my time was to be spent in prayer and contemplation. It only made things worse. The more I thought about it, the more ridiculous my life seemed. I had just wasted ten years.

"My father died during that month too, so I came back to Ireland for the funeral. My mother didn't know what to do with me. I told her I wasn't sure about being a nun anymore, but she was lost in her own grief and had nothing left over for me. In the end I couldn't bear being at home...and I definitely wasn't going to stay at the convent here in Athlone while I sorted myself out, so I went to Dublin for a few weeks. Josie offered me a place to stay. After that I went back to Australia and told Mother Superior I was going to leave the convent at the end of the term. Maybe she had dealt with this situation before and knew how futile it was to try to change my mind because I remember she didn't say anything; she just sat there with her hands folded in her lap. The order found a place for me to live, and I got another teaching job, this time at a secular school.

"Then I met Ron. He was the father of one of my pupils; we met at a parent teacher consult. I can't remember how the subject came up, but he told me he had been a priest. Suddenly, there was someone who understood what I was going through, who could reassure me that the anguish would end. We continued to meet and talk, and one thing led to another. He was a widow with a six-year-old daughter, and we ended up getting married and having two boys and two girls. He's a good man. We're both good people, just not cut out for the religious life."

"That's quite the story," I said. I had nothing to compare from my last fifty years: university, marriage, children, grandchildren, retirement, family vacations by the sea—it seemed so ordinary by comparison. But I wouldn't have wanted her life. Even though I'm not a practicing Catholic anymore, I can see how devastating it must have been for her. To be a "Bride of Christ" and then have him turn his back on you....

We finished up our drinks and walked back to the hotel. Nuala went to her room to freshen up while I went to see the room where we would have dinner that evening. There were eighteen of us and I had drawn up a seating plan for the table, alternating girls from the east half of the country with those from the west. There would be a centerpiece—two candles and a silver ribbon draped at their base with the names of the two girls who had died. Everyone was to meet in the hotel bar around six that evening, dinner would be served at half-past seven, and the hotel management promised they'd keep the bar open as late as we wanted.

I was the last person to arrive at the bar. Because I had just read each of their names, I had a mental image of every girl, but now as I approached a group of mostly grey-haired, older women, for a moment I thought I was at the wrong party. In my mind were the faces I remembered from our last day at boarding school, seventeen-year-olds with their whole lives ahead of them. Nuala saw me hesitate and came rushing over and pulled me into the group.

"Isn't she wonderful," she said with a flourish of her hand. "Our Head Girl who organized everything!"

The meal was indifferent, but no one seemed to care. The waitstaff were attentive, and by now everyone had quite a lot to drink. I tapped a fork against my water glass and in the brief silence that followed, raised a toast to those who were present as well as those who couldn't make it to the reunion, reciting their names one by one. I finished with a toast to the two girls who were gone forever. The slightly somber tone that ensued lasted barely a minute before the living returned to their animated conversations. Between the main course and dessert, one of the girls raised her voice and suggested that we all move two places to our left so that we would have a new person facing us at the long narrow table. It seemed a good idea to me, and I got up to move as did a few of the other girls. I was surprised when neither Josie nor Nuala moved. They were seated at opposite ends of the table, and I presumed they would want to chat.

Josie struggled to her feet and with a shout that could be heard throughout the room said, "I don't mind moving as long as I don't have to sit beside *her. She* slept with my husband."

All eyes followed her finger, which was pointing at Nuala.

Josie sat back down, picked up her wine glass and with a dramatic gesture, drained it. For maybe twenty seconds there was total silence at the table. Then, amazingly, the conversation resumed as if nothing had happened. Another hour came and went, and by now the staff were getting restless, so I shooed everyone off to the bar and headed for my room, exhausted, but at the same time exhilarated. As far as I could tell, the reunion had been a great success.

One by one the women wandered into the dining room the following morning, many of them showing the effects of a late night at the hotel bar, which I was told had closed around three in the morning. I left the dining room for a few minutes to see about paying the bill and noticed Josie and Nuala sitting together on a bench by the elevator, their heads almost touching. Reassured that they had finally had a chance to catch up, I walked past them to the manager's office. Neither of them looked up as I passed.

§

I had agreed to drop Nuala at Dublin airport and was looking forward to the drive back to the city. We would deconstruct the evening, gossip about the girls, and congratulate ourselves on a thoroughly successful event.

"I thought that went well," I said as we merged onto the M6 motorway. "And I'm glad you got a chance to finally talk with Josie."

Nuala was silent. I glanced over at her and was surprised to see a tear rolling down her cheek.

"What's wrong?"

"I wasn't going to tell you."

I noticed that she was twisting the gold band on her ring finger.

"It's true what Josie said last night. I slept with her husband." Nuala sighed.

I was confused. As far as I knew, Nuala hadn't been back to Ireland since Josie got married.

"But you couldn't have—you weren't here," I said dismissively. "Besides, she was totally drunk last night. None of us believed her."

"Remember I told you that I came home for my Father's funeral? It happened then. I couldn't bear to stay in the house with my mother in Cork so I came up to Dublin. Josie used to write to me when I was in Africa, and she kept it up when I went to Australia. So it was only natural that she'd offer me a bed in her flat. She was doing a midwifery rotation at St. Vincent's Hospital, working all sorts of hours so I had the place to myself, more or less. She and Rory had been dating for a couple of years—he was a doctor at the hospital—and he used to come around to the flat almost every evening. I'm not making an excuse, but I was totally messed up at that time. All the girls I went to school with had these other lives—normal lives, with boyfriends and fiancés and marriage and children... and sex. And I had nothing. I felt I had wasted ten years of my life and I wanted to catch up. One evening I asked him to kiss me. I'd never been kissed. Not properly. Once, by my cousin, but we were just kids." She gave a tiny laugh.

"Rory was a good-looking fellow, and over the course of several evenings thrust into each other's company I thought there was a spark between us. One thing led to another and..." She shrugged. "Afterwards, I made him swear he would never tell Josie. But he must have. I suppose he couldn't bring himself to go through with the wedding unless he told her everything. Her letters stopped coming after that. I thought about writing to her, apologizing, saying it wasn't Rory's fault. But I wasn't sorry. I'd just lost ten years of my life, given them away to something I no longer believed in. I was so angry...with myself, the Church...everyone."

Her voice had risen, and she almost shouted the last few words. She slumped back into the seat and stared ahead; out of the corner of my eye I could see her chest heaving. We drove in silence for several miles, each of us lost in the past.

Finally, I blurted out, "But that was fifty years ago for heaven's sake. We all did stupid things when we were young."

Nuala let out a long sigh. "Josie told me this morning she's never forgiven me and never will. She said that I ruined her life."

"I don't see how," I said in a voice that reminded me of my mother when she used to try to talk sense into me.

"She's been married to the same man for almost fifty years. Her children did well for themselves—one of them is a doctor, and I heard her say last night she has five grandchildren. The whole family goes to their holiday place in the south of Spain every year at Christmas. What does she have to complain about?"

"Rory is an alcoholic. Josie had breast cancer a few years ago and still has a lot of problems with side-effects from the chemo and radiation. Her other son is bipolar and one of the grandchildren has ADD."

She turned to face at me, and I was glad I had to

concentrate on the traffic and could avoid her gaze. She was sobbing now.

"I felt as if she were pouring all of her life's misery and disappointment into a chalice and handing it to me."

I chose my words carefully. "You don't have to drink it."

"No...but I can't ignore it either."

We didn't speak for the remainder of the journey. I dropped her at the airport terminal. She thanked me again and we hugged briefly. Barely thirty hours had elapsed, but the energetic Sports Captain had been erased; instead, a tired, grey-haired, old lady walked slowly towards the entrance.

I couldn't face going home so I decided to stop off at my daughter's house. James would be just about to go to bed and afterwards, Laura and I could have a chat. I would tell her the highlights of the reunion and somehow manage to transform the tragedy into a comedy of sorts.

James rushed to greet me with a yelp of pleasure, wrapping his tiny arms around my thighs. He let go and ran to the bedroom, his feet making a soft padding sound. A moment later he returned, brandishing the wand.

"Maxie, Maxie," he shouted, jumping up and down.

Before Laura could intervene, I took the wand from his pudgy little hand and waved it in a wide circle above my head like the fairy godmother in *Cinderella*.

"Remissio."

James reached both arms up towards the wand, stuttering the word I had just spoken.

"Misso, Misso."

I knelt down beside him and whispered, "It's a new spell. It means forgiveness."

The Boys' Club

Her eyes darted back and forth along the row of dials, then focused on the altimeter. With a shock she saw that the small plane had descended by three hundred feet.

"Fly the plane, Karen!" The rebuke came from the right seat.

She turned her head, but the seat was empty. A sob welled up in her throat. At that moment she would have given anything to see Willy's bulky shape. He had been a demanding flight instructor, always on her case and accepting nothing short of perfection. Yet, thanks to his relentless badgering she had soloed after ten hours and passed her flight test on the first try. That was three years ago, and since then she had dutifully kept her license current with the required three take-offs and landings every ninety days.

The momentary distraction was a sharp reminder that any mistake on this flight could be fatal. Three hundred feet wasn't much in the flat Illinois landscape—except that outside it was now pitch black. A glance at the Loran radio navigation system showed that she was still on course for Middleton airport in Wisconsin. Adjusting the propeller pitch and pushing slightly on the throttle, she pulled back gingerly on the yoke and listened as the engine registered the climb. She shifted slightly, trying to relax her shoulders but they resisted. Fear had lodged in every corner of her body, leaving her mouth dry and her stomach tense. She tried to pinpoint exactly when or where she had made the mistake that had led to this state of affairs. There were several, but it all went back to joining the flying club. Six months earlier an old friend had asked if she was interested in buying his membership in the Verona Flying Club. He was moving to Arizona where, he assured her, the skies were always clear and the visibility unlimited.

"It's a well-run club," Bob assured her. "Most of the guys—there are fifteen members in the club—are doctors and lawyers so there's never any problem with money for fuel, repairs, maintenance...those sorts of things. The club owns two four-seater Cessnas—one with fixed gear, one retractable—and they rent a hangar at the Middleton airport." He paused for a moment, then chuckled.

"You'll be the first woman in the club. Now there's a change." He gave her a knowing look. "For the better, of course," he added with a reassuring smile.

The buy-in price, five thousand dollars, was more

than she wanted to spend, but Bob reminded her that she would actually own a piece of each airplane, even if it was only one-fifteenth. Moreover, he was diligent to point out that the club hourly rental rates were the same as she was currently paying for the tiny two-seater Cessna she flew regularly.

"The best part is that you can sign out a plane for up to a week, and you only pay for the hours you fly. You could go anywhere...the sky's the limit." He laughed at his unexpected witticism.

"Let's fly to Reedsburg for lunch on Thursday. It'll give you an idea of how things work in the club. I can show you the hangar, the planes, and how to get them out onto the ramp."

That Thursday she and Bob drove to the airport and parked beside one of several large, metal hangars that flanked the runway. With the flick of a switch, the massive grey door folded upwards, revealing two airplanes. While she watched, Bob attached an electric tug to the nose wheel of a sleek-looking, yellow Cessna Cardinal and maneuvered it past the frumpier Cessna Skylark and out into the sunshine. Within five minutes they had taken off from the paved runway and were flying west, beneath them a sea of corn fields punctuated by red barns and dark blue silos. Half an hour later they landed at a small rural airstrip and walked over to a Nissen hut where two enterprising local women ran a small restaurant. The lunch spot, Bob informed her, was popular not just with local farmers but also helicopter crews from the nearby Air Force base, as well as private pilots like him. She felt as if she had been let in on a carefully-guarded secret and given a glimpse into another world. By the end of that lunch, she had agreed to buy Bob's share in the flying club.

On the way back from Reedsburg, he suggested that she fly in the left seat, taking over as pilot-in-command.

"You might as well start to become familiar with the plane," he said. "The biggest difference between this and the one you're used to flying is the retractable landing gear. Just remember to make sure the gear is down and locked. Otherwise, it could be a very expensive mistake and the guys will never let you forget it." He laughed.

"Oh, and one more thing—Cardinals tend to float. Just as you're about to land, the ground seems to fall out from under you. You sort of have to drive the plane onto the runway as opposed to letting it flare and settle. Don't worry, you'll get used to it," he added reassuringly.

The following week she mailed a check to Bob. Her ownership and insurance documents took a few more weeks, but eventually she received a bulky envelope from the club secretary with all of the paperwork. There was a brief note reminding her that she needed to get checked out in each of the planes by a certified flight instructor before she could fly solo. After that, the club members would take a formal vote on her membership.

Karen dressed carefully for her first club meeting. She debated wearing heels with the outfit—tailored trousers, a silk shirt, and a stylish jacket—but in the end decided on flats. She arrived ten minutes early to the meeting room in the basement of a local bank, in time to observe an older man positioning long narrow tables to form a square. He paused for a moment to introduce himself as the club secretary, shook her hand, then returned to his task while she watched, uncertain whether she should offer to help him.

"Sit anywhere you like," he said with a wave of his hand.

Taking the seat facing him, she watched as he arranged his papers, feeling like an errant school child called up in front of the principal. Over the course of the next twenty minutes a dozen or so men, their ages ranging from late forties to early seventies, filed into the room. They greeted each other warmly, and then, as each in turn noticed her, they came over to introduce themselves. She made an effort to remember their names, focusing on each person, repeating the name aloud, and trying to link it to something she already knew. Tom, John, Ralph, Ed, Nathan, Michael, Jim...she suppressed an urge to write the names down.

The club president called the meeting to order, and she was reassured to see all hands raised in assent when her membership was proposed. The next item of business was whether the club would buy a new piece of avionics for the Cessna Cardinal. Listening to the discussion, she was reminded of a group of boys talking excitedly amongst themselves about the latest cool gadgets. It didn't matter whether they were discussing bicycles or cars, boats or airplanes, or even computers, the interplay was always the same, with everyone showcasing their precious nuggets of information. When the club president called for a vote, she decided to abstain, shrugging her shoulders when he made eye contact with her. In the end the vote was unanimous.

The business part of the meeting completed, people began to chat amongst themselves in groups of two or three. It wasn't that they deliberately excluded her, but nobody made any effort to include her in their conversations. Tucking her purse under her arm, she made for the door. Just as she was about to open it the club secretary called out to her.

"You're all set, Karen. Just give me a call when you want to schedule one of the planes," he said, then turned back to his friends.

Over the next few weeks she checked out each of the planes, flying them for a couple of hours at a time over the skies of south-western Wisconsin, followed by practice landings at Middleton airport. Gradually she came to know their idiosyncrasies. The Skylark reminded her of the first car she had owned, a Toyota Corolla—solid and reliable. The Cardinal was more like a sports car—a complex machine that demanded one's full attention.

At subsequent club meetings she forced herself to stay after the business discussion, insinuating herself into conversations, listening as the men compared notes on trips they had flown in the previous few months. Many of these stories had a "triumph over adversity" theme— unexpected weather, crosswind landings, mechanical or electrical issues—and she enjoyed listening to them. Inevitably, someone would turn to her and ask, "Why don't you take one of the planes and *go* somewhere, Karen. It's all very well boring holes in the sky around here but the real advantage of being in this club is that you can take a plane and go away for a few days." Her stock reply was that she was too busy with work. The reality was that she was afraid.

The opportunity came in November. Her professional organization was holding its annual meeting in St. Louis, a six-hour drive, but a mere two hours if she flew there herself. Her heart was thumping as she called the club secretary to reserve the Cardinal, trying to sound casual.

"You're lucky," he said. "Nobody has it signed out for that week, but Tom is down for the following one. Make sure you have it back on time."

Nearing the departure date, she checked the weather obsessively, mindful of her self-imposed limits—ten-thousand-foot ceilings and fifteen-knot crosswinds. Her destination was St. Charles County airport, a place not unlike Middleton airport, with paved north-south and east-west runways, a fixed-base operation and maintenance facility, and tie-downs for small aircraft.

From takeoff to landing, the flight to St. Louis went perfectly. At St. Charles airport she taxied the plane to the ramp, shut down the engine, and handed the keys to the attendant with a tiny flourish. She felt magnificent.

"This is a first for me—picking up a lady pilot here— and I sure am impressed," the elderly taxi driver said as he held the door of the cab open for her. "Weren't you at all scared?"

She thought about his question for a moment. If she were honest, she had been terrified for most of the flight.

"A little, but I've been flying for three years. I'm well-trained," she said, noting her self-assured tone.

She used to dread these annual meetings. Her profession was dominated by men who, whether through ignorance or intent, always managed to make her feel insignificant. This time felt utterly different. Her self-perceived inadequacies seemed to fade, replaced by a new feeling of confidence. She found that she was looking forward to the next three days.

That evening at the opening reception, a man from the regional office, who she knew slightly, asked whether she had driven from Wisconsin.

"No. I flew here...myself. I'm a pilot."

She watched as comprehension dawned on his face, followed by a look of incredulity.

"No way!" he said, his eyes opening wide.

Turning to the rest of the group he announced loudly, "Hey guys. This lady flew here in her own plane."

Suddenly, she was the center of attention, and for once she didn't mind their eyes dropping to her breasts where her name tag hung. This time they actually wanted to know her name.

On the morning of her departure, the weather was CAVU, the acronym used by pilots for ceiling and visibility unlimited. A front was approaching from the plains but not due to arrive in Wisconsin until later that night. She had all day to get home. From the fixed-base operator at St. Charles airport she called flight services and filed her flight plan. The plane had been refueled, but nonetheless she checked the level in the wing tanks and took a sample looking for water in the avgas. With a last visual inspection as she walked around the plane, she climbed up into the cockpit and closed the door, pushing the lever fully forward to engage the lock. Her flight checklist complete, she primed and started the engine, radioed her position and intentions, and taxied to the active runway. Pushing the throttle fully forward, the plane gathered speed as it traveled down the centerline, smoothly lifting off when she applied back pressure on the yoke. She could feel the tension in her body begin to relax.

Suddenly, there was a "whoosh" and the plane shuddered. Her eyes darted back and forth between the gauges. The engine rpm was stable and she was gaining altitude, but something was wrong. With a rising sense of panic, she searched for the source of the loud noise that filled the cockpit. Looking down to her left, she could see the ground through a three-inch gap that had opened up between the door and the fuselage. Somehow the door had opened.

Fly the plane. These three words were uppermost in her mind as she pulled back on the throttle, leveling the plane off at the pattern altitude. She radioed her intentions hurriedly to anyone who might be listening—she had an emergency and was returning to the airport immediately.

The next five hours drained every drop of confidence she had accumulated over the previous four days. The mechanic made it clear that she would have to wait her turn; he was busy with another plane, so she sat in the lounge of the fixed-base operator, idly paging through old copies of flying magazines. Alternately glancing at the clock and looking outside at the weather, she waited. Every half hour she walked back to the maintenance hangar to check on the mechanic's progress. When he finally took the interior panel off the door frame, he found that the door handle had stripped out. He showed her what must have happened, sliding the door handle onto the ribbed stem where it rotated ineffectively. Then he attached a vice grip to the stem and demonstrated that the actual locking mechanism was still working.

"You just need a new stem. But I don't have a replacement in stock," he told her, shaking his head. "It'll be several days before I can get one." He looked at her, waiting for her response.

She weighed her options. If she could borrow the mechanic's vice grips, perhaps she could lock the door and continue with her flight plan. The weather was still clear, the front four hours out. If she left immediately, she could get back to Wisconsin before dark. She asked to borrow the tool, assuring him she would mail it back, but he didn't like that idea. After a considerable harangue, he agreed to sell her the tool, adding that he took no responsibility for what she was about to do.

The minutes ticked by as he finished up the requisite paperwork. Then she had to go back to the office to file a revised flight plan, causing further delay. Finally, with barely two hours left before darkness, she took off from the airport. Staring down at the grimy metal wrench, she prayed that it would work. In the back of her mind nestled a grim fact. The elegant design of the Cardinal had been achieved by removing the wing struts and enlarging the doors—doors that when closed became an integral part of the airframe and without which the airplane was no longer airworthy. If the door popped open, the plane could break up in flight.

She watched the bank of clouds approaching from the west, contrasting sharply against the clear sky above her. Suspended in this increasingly grey landscape, fear lodged in her chest. One by one she went over the choices she had made. Considered individually, each one was logical, but together they added up to a classic case of "get-home-itis" syndrome, the most common cause of death among private pilots.

Two hours seemed like an eternity. She checked and rechecked her altimeter and compass, seeking the reassurance that she was going in the right direction and unlikely to collide with any tall obstructions. The radio was silent so she briefly switched to a different frequency, searching for a voice—any voice—to be reassured that it was working. She had never felt so utterly alone. A few lights twinkled below in the now total blackness, reminding her that for the first time ever, she would have to land at Middleton airport in the dark. All of her previous practice "nighttime" landings had been undertaken during the hour after sunset, which fulfilled the requirements for maintaining her license but bore little resemblance to the real thing. Suddenly, the radio crackled to life, and her heart leapt as she heard the call sign for her airplane. The regional airspace controller at Chicago Center informed her that she was leaving their airspace and could now resume her own navigation. In other words, from here on she was on her own.

Five miles from Middleton airport she dialed in the Unicom frequency and keyed the microphone button. Peering into the darkness ahead, she searched for the runway lights, praying that they were operational. A tiny strip of white appeared in the distance, faint as a line of chalk on a dusty blackboard. A wave of relief swept over her, but almost immediately it was smothered by the enormity of the task that lay ahead. Easing back on the throttle, she descended to pattern altitude, one thousand feet above the airport. Adjusting the propeller pitch and slowing the plane down, she flipped the toggle switch that activated the landing gear. A reassuring whirring sound was followed by a click as the gear locked into place and a green light appeared on the dash. Keeping an eye on the airspeed, she lined the plane up for runway 28. Although she couldn't see a wind indicator, any wind from the approaching front would be coming from the west, she reasoned. Lowering the flaps, she eased back on the throttle and lined the plane up between the parallel row of runway lights. A quick glance at the airspeed indicator showed she was approaching stall speed, and she eased back on the yoke, anticipating the moment of touchdown. The plane refused to drop. Instead, it floated above the runway as the line of lights ahead of her contracted. With a sickening feeling she realized she was going to crash.

"Fly the plane, Karen." It was Willy's voice, steady and commanding.

How many times in a practice landing had he surprised her by shouting, "Go around! There's a deer on the runway."

In an instant, she rammed the throttle forward and swiped the flap switch upward. The engine roared to life, and she resisted the urge to pull back on the yoke; she didn't have sufficient airspeed to climb just yet. For a brief moment she considered retracting the landing gear—it would reduce drag—but decided to keep the gear down. It would be one less thing to worry about on the next attempt. As the plane began to climb, she took a quick look over her left shoulder. She didn't want to lose sight of the runway lights.

"You are well-trained. You know how to do this," she said aloud, reminding herself that she had made this approach dozens of times in the past. But another scenario wormed its way into her head. She would touch down too close to the end of the runway, plough into the cornfield that lay beyond, and bury the propeller in the dirt—a very expensive mistake. Or worse, the plane would somersault and end up crumpled on its back. The fuel tanks were at least half full. Hanging upside down from her harness in the dark, would she be able to get out in time if a fire started? There were so many ways for this to end up badly.

Loosening the death grip she had on the yoke, she flexed her fingers, took a deep breath, and checked again for the landing lights. As if Willy were sitting beside her, she began to describe each action systematically. "Turning onto the base leg of the approach, airspeed one hundred knots, altitude thirteen hundred feet." The sound of her voice was oddly reassuring. "Turning onto final, lined up with the runway lights, landing gear down, flaps ten degrees, airspeed eighty knots, altitude twelve hundred feet..."

Two minutes later she touched down. Easing on the brakes, she brought the plane to a full stop at the end of the runway and sat for several minutes, allowing the thumping in her chest to subside. She was alive. Her hands still gripped the yoke, and she had to will them to relax. Tears welled up and spilled onto her cheeks. She began to sob.

Taxiing to the maintenance hangar, she shut down the engine and climbed out the passenger door. Her legs felt wobbly, like a newborn foal taking its first steps. Leaving the keys in the drop box at the hangar, she walked slowly to her car, relishing the solidity of the tarmac. Just as she was about to start the engine, a few drops of rain dotted the windscreen.

The following morning she called the club secretary and told him about the door handle.

"The Cardinal is in the maintenance hangar at Middleton airport, but I just talked to them and they won't be able to get the part for another week," Karen explained.

"So the plane is back?"

Karen thought she detected a note of surprise in his voice.

"Tell Tom I'm sorry," she said. "I know he wanted the plane for next week."

"It's not your fault," the secretary replied. "Could have happened to anyone."

"I left the vice grips in the plane. They worked fine. He could still go if he wanted to," she suggested

"Nah. He wouldn't risk it."

Those words stayed with her for a long time. Tom, who had hundreds of hours of flight time logged, wouldn't risk flying the Cardinal with a vice grips holding the door closed. But *she* had. Looking at her decision objectively, she had been stupid and reckless, and had anything gone wrong she would have died. It was a sobering thought.

Yet, even as she acknowledged this, another part of her brain was secretly elated. At the next meeting of the flying club she would have a story to tell.

Here Lies Janet Cowles

The hand-made sign had been nailed to a wooden post that marked the junction of Skunk Hollow and Bluegrass Road. The crudely cut three-quarter-inch particle board, with its coat of white paint highlighting the imperfections in the man-made surface, gave it the appearance of a child's school project. The shape was reminiscent of a Celtic cross and was clearly meant to represent a gravestone. An inscription was painted on it in crooked, blue letters surrounded by small hearts.

Here Lies
Janet Cowles
1937-1992
R.I.P.

The sign had been there for easily a year, and

I still didn't know who Janet Cowles was. That bugged me. I knew most of my neighbors and there was nobody called Cowles on Skunk Hollow or Bluegrass Road. Why someone would go to the trouble of nailing the sign to that post was a mystery, and even more of a puzzle was why someone would rip it down and throw it into the weeds shortly after it had been put up. Within a week the sign was replaced, and yet barely a month later the entire post was uprooted, leaving a conspicuous hole in the ground. It would have taken a pickup truck and a length of chain to accomplish such vandalism, and I wondered who amongst my neighbors had been so angry. In the final act of this tit-for-tat drama, when the county erected a new road sign, a freshly-painted grave marker had been nailed to the wooden post within a couple days. That's when I began my search for Janet Cowles.

Skunk Hollow and Bluegrass Road marked the northwest corner of a township about fifty miles from Iowa City. The township records had been digitized and were easy to access at our local library. Nonetheless, even with generous margins around the years 1937 and 1992, I found no mention of Janet Cowles—no births or deaths with that name. Another possibility I considered was a road accident at the corner, and I spent several days scouring the local newspapers on microfilm, again with no success. Finally, I tried Google with a myriad of different search terms, but the information giant failed me.

Since retiring I've taken to walking four or five miles each day. The dog needed a bit of exercise, so she and I headed out each morning, varying our route as much as we could. The road through the valley stretched four miles from east to west, with another going north to join the state highway. Skunk Hollow was an afterthought as roads go, a dead end leading to a scattering of houses nestled at the base of steep, wooded hillsides. I could make an accurate count but it was not worth the effort; let's just say there were forty or so households in the valley, and I was on passing acquaintance with many of my neighbors. So, I made it a point that each time I met one of them, I would ask if they knew anything about the grave marker—for that was what I assumed it was—or the name Janet Cowles. It was an interesting project for many reasons, not least that it gave me an opportunity to talk to someone during the day. I am seventy-six years of age, and since my wife died six years ago, I had become a bit of a hermit. Our daughter moved out of state after she graduated from college; rural Iowa cannot compete with the west coast when you are young.

I was surprised to discover that at least half of my neighbors had never noticed the sign, and several who had seen it weren't the least bit curious as to its origins. A few of the older folks who have lived in the valley for most of their lives offered "If so-and-so were alive, *she'd* know," as if this was useful information. I had almost given up when something happened that changed everything.

It was in late May, one of those magnificent mornings, when the world feels as if it has been resurrected. A series of thunderstorms had passed through the day before and everything looked and smelled fresh and clean. You could almost hear the grass growing, trees budding out, insects hatching. Lucy and I set out for our walk after breakfast. She was getting slower, but she had all the instincts of a Labrador and would follow her nose, indifferent to my commands to "heel." I know she should have been on a leash, but there was not much traffic in the valley, and she was fairly savvy when it came to avoiding passing cars, crouching in the ditch by the side of the road until they passed.

We were going by Rasta John's place when something caught her attention and she took off, squeezing through a gap in his fence and disappearing somewhere behind the derelict barn. The tin roof was mostly intact but you could see the skeleton of timber support posts through gaps in the wood siding. I remembered thinking that the whole structure looked as if it was holding its breath, bracing for the storm that would finally demolish it. When Lucy didn't reappear, I began to call her name, my tone more insistent with each repetition. I must have spent five minutes or more shouting, my voice getting weaker as my irritation increased. Maybe it was all the yelling, but I suddenly felt light-headed. The next thing I knew I was lying on the ground and Rasta John was leaning over me. I must have struggled to sit upright because he squatted down and helped me maneuver into a position where I could lean against the fence.

"I'm just going to get a glass of water," he said. "Don't move. I'll be back in a minute."

I sat there obediently, slumped against the wire mesh, not confident enough in my legs to try to stand up. I must have closed my eyes, for I got a bit of a shock when a moist wet tongue licked my face. Lucy had returned, unapologetic, and her foul breath was like a vial of smelling salts. I pushed her away.

"Here. Drink this," Rasta John said, thrusting a glass towards me with his right hand and patting the dog with his left.

The water was ice cold, and I could feel it making its way down my throat and into my stomach.

"I'm so sorry...."

"Let me help you get up."

We spoke at the same time, my apology muffling his offer to help. I grabbed his outstretched hand and got to my feet but almost immediately began to sink down. John didn't hesitate, wrapping his arm around my waist and pulling my own arm around his neck. He was surprisingly strong for someone who looked to be nearly as old as me.

"Let's go inside," he said. "You can decide then if you want me to call an ambulance."

Rasta John isn't his real name. I overheard someone calling him that once; he has distinctive grey dreadlocks and a long, shaggy beard. We don't know each other—at least, we've never been introduced formally. Occasionally I'd see him working in his garden and wave, one of those vague waves where you don't really expect the person to wave back, but just in case, you want to have your gesture of friendliness established first. Someone told me he had been in Vietnam, and I presumed he was one of those damaged veterans who chose to retreat from society and a country that had failed them.

We walked about fifty yards to John's house, a trailer that was parked behind the barn and flanked by two corrugated metal sheds. Anyone glancing at the neglected farmyard would never suspect that someone lived there, although on my winter walks I had noticed a thin plume of smoke coming from somewhere in that area. John guided me up the step—a sturdy log—and into the trailer. He helped me to a worn leather recliner, releasing his grip and lowering me carefully into the chair. Lucy followed us inside and slumped at my feet with a satisfied sigh.

Before I could apologize for her behavior, John said, "She's fine there. Don't worry—I like dogs. They don't talk back."

To my way of thinking, dreadlocks are the hallmark of someone who has let themselves go, and I expected the trailer to be grimy, with a pile of dirty dishes in the sink and unwashed pots on the stove. I admit my own house is a little untidy, but stacks of books on the floor are a sign of curiosity, not sloth. To my surprise John's trailer was orderly and clean. Looking past the table, I could see that the bed was made, its corners pulled taut with military precision.

"What do you think? Should I call an ambulance?" he asked. His voice sounded gravelly as if he wasn't accustomed to talking.

"No, I'm fine. Just give me a couple more minutes and I'll be on my way."

"I've some coffee made." He nodded in the direction of the counter where an old-fashioned thermos flask stood. "I was having a cup when I heard you shouting."

Without waiting for an answer, he took a mug from the cupboard above the sink and poured a cup.

"Sugar? I don't have any milk. Or something stronger?"

"Black is fine," I said.

I expected a cup of bitter liquid, but the coffee was

surprisingly good, making me question my original opinion of Rasta John. In fact, everything in his trailer begged questions, from the neatness of the room to the book titles on the shelf across from where I was sitting. Some of those titles were on my own shelves.

I felt awkward occupying the only comfortable seat in the trailer, but John didn't seem to mind, instead, sitting on a straight-backed chair by the small table. By way of making conversation, I started to talk about COVID-19 and how strange the world had become in the past few weeks. We agreed that the pandemic hadn't made much difference to us. After all, we lived alone in a valley far removed from mainstream life, with infrequent trips to the local town.

Something about the intimate space encouraged me to talk, and I found myself telling John about my life in Iowa City before retiring here. He listened, nodding occasionally as if in agreement, although I couldn't imagine any commonality in our lives. All the same, I found myself looking past his dreadlocks and grimy fingernails, his worn shirt and bare feet, and began to think of him as a person and not just a stereotype. He told me he had been a medic in Vietnam, mostly assigned to helicopters. As he described the work, his eyes darted back and forth, and I noticed that his hands shook. He saw me looking at them and grasped them firmly together to stop the tremor.

"I was 4F," I offered, adding "I don't hear well. Something to do with streptomycin for a bacterial infection as a child. I lip read, but that wouldn't have worked in Vietnam."

I had told this story many times, and it was always

met with sympathy. But this time it sounded flat, as if I could have done something else, something worthwhile. For a while John didn't say anything, and we sat in silence, each of us alone with our memories of that time. After a few minutes I stood up carefully. My legs had some strength, enough to take me home, I thought. Lucy got up too and shook herself in anticipation.

Almost as an afterthought I said, "Say, you don't know anything about that sign on the corner, do you? Janet Cowles. I can't find any information about her so I'm asking everyone I meet in the valley. It's strange, but nobody seems to know who she was. She must have meant something to someone around here, especially as the sign has been replaced a couple of times. It's been repainted too."

His voice was a whisper when he replied and I had to strain to hear what he said.

"She was my mother."

Sometimes you find yourself at a loss for words. I just nodded my head, all the while trying to come up with something appropriate to say. I decided to take a chance.

"Tell me about her," I said, trying to convey in those four words that I genuinely wanted to know about her and why he had made such an effort to keep her memory alive. I could feel his hesitation, like a skittish horse when you offer a handful of oats.

"It's a long story," he said.

By way of encouragement I sat back on the recliner and took up my coffee cup, not quite emptied.

"I've got time," I said.

With that uncanny prescience that dogs seem to

possess, Lucy lay down at my feet and gave a gentle sigh. Without asking, John picked up the flask, poured more coffee into our cups, and added a shot of brandy from a bottle he took from a cupboard above the refrigerator. Returning to the chair, he looked down at his gnarled hands as if for reassurance.

"She grew up here—in that house over there." He gestured in the direction of a two-story house on the other side of the barn that had been part of the original farmstead at one time. Seeing the puzzled expression on my face, he added, "Cowles was her married name. Or maybe they never married, but she took his name, in any case. I don't know why—he was a bastard. I brought her ashes back and scattered them here, 'cause this is where it all began. She liked this place...used to talk about her childhood here, walking to school...good times. But then it all ended." He paused for a sip of coffee before resuming.

"I put up the sign so they'd be reminded."

I didn't understand what he was trying to tell me. John, meanwhile, seemed lost in his own thoughts. He clenched and unclenched his jaw, a muscle in his throat moving rhythmically. I waited for a couple of minutes, then prompted him again.

"Reminded of what?"

His head shot up, and he looked directly at me.

"Where he raped her. That's where it happened, or near enough. She was walking home from school when he stopped his truck and got out. He pulled her into the woods across the road from the marsh and raped her. She was seventeen. He did it again a week later, and after that a bunch more times. He'd follow her home from school, sometimes even from church."

In that tiny cramped space, I felt like an intruder and inwardly regretted my stubborn curiosity. Suddenly, he shook his head roughly from side to side, his dreadlocks moving like a tangle of writhing snakes. When he spoke again, his voice was anguished.

"It was old man Hansen. She went to school with his kids, for God's sake."

"Why didn't she tell someone?" I blurted out. The look he gave me was harrowing.

"Who could she tell? Her parents? Hanson and his wife were their friends; they lived on the next farm. He warned her that if she said anything, he'd kill her. He said nobody would ever believe her. After all, he was a respectable farmer, a deacon in the local church who knew his Bible. When she told him she was pregnant, he gave her a few hundred dollars—enough for a bus ticket to somewhere far away from here. She went to Las Vegas. That's where I was born." He gave a shrug. "In the beginning he used to send her money. But after a few years that dried up. I think he died. I hope he went straight to hell."

He spat out the words.

"She managed okay for a while, but money was always tight. She was a good-looking woman in her early twenties and...well, it was easy to make money in Vegas in those days. No questions asked, if you know what I mean. Then she hooked up with my stepfather—another brute who couldn't keep his dick to himself. He gave her

AIDS, and by the time she found out, he was long gone. By then I was gone too; I signed up even before the lottery.

"After Vietnam I hung around Southeast Asia for a few years. Came back the long way 'round, working on yachts. The money wasn't great, but I didn't need much. The next few years were mostly in the Caribbean doing this and that. For a few years I ferried yachts up the east coast for people before hurricane season set in or down the Mississippi from Chicago to the Gulf. Those were good times. After that I did a spell on an oil rig off Galveston. It wasn't much of a life but the money made it worthwhile.

"Somewhere in there I went back to Vegas to see my Mom. She was sick, real sick—I could see that, but she didn't want to go to a doctor. Said it would cost too much. That's when she told me about Evan Hansen—what he had done. I was all set to come back here and kill him but he was already dead. I stayed with her for the last few months. She had nobody else.

"She was close to the end when out of nowhere a lawyer contacts her to say she's inherited a farm in Iowa. She hadn't gone back in all those years, but she'd send a postcard to her folks every so often, just so they'd know she was still alive. I don't know how the lawyer tracked her down, but he managed it somehow. It's not that easy to live under the radar in this country. Easy enough in Southeast Asia, but not here. Still, I do my best. Most people don't know there's anyone living back here. Suits me fine.

"There was nothing keeping me in Vegas, and Iowa sounded as good a place as any. I put the house on the market—didn't need a house, and the money I got for it would keep me going for years. But I kept the land. There's something about owning a bit of land..." His voice trailed off. "You can always feed yourself," he added with a conviction born of a lifetime of living on the margin.

"Even though they're just the other side of the barn, I don't have anything to do with the folks who bought the house. Don't have anything to do with anyone around here...except the Hansens. When I came back and set myself up in this trailer, the Hansen boys came by wanting to know if I was interested in selling off some land. They inherited their grandfather's farm. That's when I told them to fuck off. Did they expect me to sell out to the family who destroyed my mother's life? Okay, it was their grandfather, not them. But it doesn't matter."

He gave a harsh laugh.

"You should have seen the expression on their faces when I let on that Evan was my father. They began to tell me what a decent, God-fearing man their grandfather had been—that he'd never do anything like that. 'Do you want me to take a DNA test?' I asked. That shut them up. Because if I was right, I'd be their uncle. Who knows, I might even have a claim on their farm.

"Everybody around here knew what sort of a man Hansen was. My mother wasn't the only girl he got his hands on. But it was always hushed up. After all, Hansens were the big farmers around here; they ran the show, and nobody dared challenge them. So I put the sign up to remind those two, and everyone else who knows them, that their grandfather was a monster. And when they pulled the sign down, I told them I'd kill both of them if they touched it again. I've done a lot worse than that in 'Nam. It wouldn't cost me a thought."

He stood up abruptly, drained his coffee cup, and rinsed it out.

"Are you okay to go home now?"

It wasn't really a question. I knew he wanted me to leave. He had shared his story with me, and as it lingered in the space around us, I sensed he was beginning to regret his candor.

When I stepped out of the trailer, the eastern sky was filled with puffy cumulus clouds behind which stretched an expanse of blue. Another brief storm had passed through, although oddly enough I don't remember hearing rain. There were new puddles on the road, and Lucy ran ahead, relishing the myriad of fresh smells. I trudged behind her, feeling the weight of my own life... and John's too.

I found myself thinking about John quite a lot over the next few days. I knew a few Vietnam veterans; I had visited the wall in Washington, DC, and read *Dispatches* and *The Things They Carried*. John had been damaged, although how much was caused by the war and how much originated in his mother's story was difficult to say. Regardless, he had set himself apart when he came back to live here.

In those couple of hours in his trailer, John and I had exchanged confidences that made me feel close to the man. We had found a common ground, or so I hoped. We were the same age, more or less, and had shared the same history. I imagined him stopping by my house every so often—impromptu visits. He'd cycle over from the trailer on his rickety bicycle—I'd seen it leaning against the barn—or maybe he'd just walk. It isn't far. We could sit on the screen porch and share our thoughts on the world around us. There were so many questions I wanted to ask him. Here was a man who had lived the sort of life I used to dream of as a boy. He had seen war (although I wasn't sure I envied him that experience), traveled the world, ferried boats down the Mississippi like Tom Sawyer and Huckleberry Finn, sailed the Caribbean, and had even been a roustabout on an oil rig, whereas I had spent my whole life in Iowa City working for an insurance company. I'd been out of the United States just once—to Cancun on a junket with dozens of middle-aged men just like me. I hadn't even needed a passport.

There were other questions too, of a more personal nature, and I hoped our friendship might grow to a stage where I could ask them. What had he been told about his father when he was a child? What was it like to kill someone? And the biggest question of all: How does it feel when you find out you are the child of a rape?

It was some days later when Lucy and I went by John's place on our morning walk. I was looking forward to seeing him again and hoped that he would be outside, as I didn't feel comfortable opening the gate and walking up to his trailer. Looking through the fence, I saw a figure bent over in the vegetable garden, a battered baseball cap barely covering the distinctive grey dreadlocks. I hailed him, announcing my name so that he would recognize me and adding that I wanted to thank him for his kindness the previous week. He raised an arm in the air and waved vaguely in my direction. But he didn't straighten up or pause in his task. I stood there on the roadside, waiting. Just in case he hadn't heard my name, I called out again. This time he didn't even wave, just continued to work, his dreadlocks obscuring his face.

After a few minutes I turned and walked back home, Lucy trotting behind, oblivious to the rejection. Passing the grave marker, I glanced at it. I had finally solved the mystery but there was no satisfaction, only a feeling of immense sadness—for Janet Cowles, her son, and for myself.

Acknowledgments

This book was conceived at Mary Devitt's coffeehouse in Cross Plains, Wisconsin. I had just published my first novel and wasn't quite ready to embark upon another. Instead, I decided to write a short story every month for a year. Amongst the Yoga Ladies who gather at the coffee shop were several beta readers willing to offer their input, especially as I had never written a short story before. In the end the project took fifteen months, but as it mostly coincided with the COVID-19 pandemic, there was little reason to hurry.

Thank you to my wonderful beta readers: Patricia Mullins, Valerie Burland, Ledell Zellers, Linda Barcz, Sandra Faust, Julie Horner, Deb Yapp, Susan Moss, Madhu Singh, Liz Fayram, Courtney Guenther and Tim Heggland, all of whom provided thoughtful, critical, and timely feedback as well as encouragement. Thanks to George Siede who came to my rescue with the cover images. Enormous thanks go to my editor, Christine Keleny, who has guided my writing career with her gentle but firm hand. Finally, this book is dedicated to my sister, Valerie Behan-Pelletier, who has been on this writing journey with me since childhood.

Author Biography

MARY BEHAN was formerly a professor of neuroscience. Now retired, she devotes her time to writing fiction, memoir, and short stories. Her first book, *Abbey Girls*, is a memoir she wrote with her sister, Valerie Behan, about their childhood in Ireland. Her first novel, *A Measured Thread*, set in Wisconsin and Ireland, was named a Top 100 Indie Book in 2020 as well as a Silver Medal winner in the eLit Book Awards. *The String of Pearls* was previously published in the Irish literary journal, *Crossways*. Mary lives with her husband in the Driftless Area of southwest Wisconsin. Visit her at mvbehan.com.

§

If you enjoyed this book, please consider leaving a review on your favorite website (Amazon, Goodreads...). Reviews are incredibly helpful to indie-authors like Mary.

~ Thank you